THE REVISED DEFINITIVE
EDITIONS OF THE WORKS
OF WILLIAM GERHARDIE

PRETTY CREATURES

The Works of William Gerhardie:

Novels
FUTILITY: *A Novel on Russian Themes*
THE POLYGLOTS
DOOM
PENDING HEAVEN
THE MEMOIRS OF SATAN (*with Brian Lunn*)
RESURRECTION
OF MORTAL LOVE
MY WIFE'S THE LEAST OF IT

Short Novels: collected
PRETTY CREATURES

Drama
DONNA QUIXOTE: *A Lyrical Comedy*
I WAS A KING IN BABYLON–AND YOU MAY VERY WELL
BE RIGHT: *An Implausible Comedy*
RASPUTIN: *The Ironical Tragedy*

Criticism and Biography
ANTON CHEKHOV: *A Critical Study*
MY LITERARY CREDO

Autobiography
MEMOIRS OF A POLYGLOT

Biographical History
THE ROMANOFFS

Collaborations
with Hugh Kingsmill
THE CASANOVA FABLE:
THE SUMMING UP

with Prince Leopold of Loewenstein
MEET YOURSELF:
studies in self-analysis

PRETTY CREATURES

WILLIAM GERHARDIE

PREFACE BY
MICHAEL HOLROYD

MACDONALD · LONDON

First published in 1927
Reissued in 1929
Definitive revised collected edition, 1974
Copyright © William Gerhardie, 1974
All rights reserved

Preface copyright © Michael Holroyd, 1974
ISBN 0 356 04595 1

Published by Macdonald and Co (Publishers) Ltd
St Giles House, 49/50 Poland Street, London W.1

Printed in Great Britain by
REDWOOD BURN LIMITED
Trowbridge & Esher

CONTENTS

PREFACE

MICHAEL HOLROYD

The practice of drawing analogies between different arts, so facile usually and so profitless, has real value in the case of William Gerhardie's work. For no one who knows his novels at all well can doubt the importance to Gerhardie of music, and of its significance in his fiction. Many of his chapter titles—'Contretemps with Double Bass'; 'Trio for Violin and two 'Cellos'—draw attention to this, as do his actual references to musicians: to Wagner in *My Wife's the Least of It*, for example, or, in *Memoirs of a Polyglot*, to Beethoven whose records 'initiate us into heaven'. Walter, the hero in *Of Mortal Love*, a young musician who is writing a symphonic poem, 'Of Mortal Love', in memory of his love for Dinah (which is the subject of the novel), reflects after death:

He could not understand. But music understood. Alone of all the arts, his own, music, was not to be known but understood us. It seemed to say that here, and yet not here, now, but not yet awhile, in a lucent world no longer shadowed by Time made flesh, it would all be stilled, the hope, the heartache, and the fear.

The three short novels and two short stories that together comprise *Pretty Creatures* were all written between the years 1924 and 1925, and they show Gerhardie's particular gifts in their purest form. The prose is highly compressed, stripped of all inessentials. It relies on verbs and adverbs rather than on adjectives—a cleaner, more wholesome style. In a review of *Pretty Creatures*, Arnold Bennett claimed that here was the prose style of the future: '*Car le mot c'est le Verbe et le Verbe c'est Dieu.*' Not a word is wasted; not a word that does not fit with its neighbours to contribute to a peculiar and insistent rhythm. From 'Tristan und Isolde', a most exquisite *aperçu* of Wagner's opera running correlatively with the mounting ecstasy and agony of 'der öde Tag', to 'The Big Drum', a record that every dog has his day; from 'The Vanity Bag', a truthful piece of *genre* centred on Innsbruck with its provincial setting of the Austrian parochial aristocracy, to his étude on black notes 'A Bad End', the musical significance of these pretty creatures is everywhere manifest. For, however accurately you write, however carefully you define, however logically and clearly you communicate your meaning, there is always some part of the truth that cannot be articulated, and it is this part that must be conveyed by the musical quality of the writing: the tone. In Gerhardie's tone we can catch that fluid undercurrent by which we recognize our life, because we see that he refuses to simplify existence in order to round off a story.

This musical significance also tells us what not to look for in Gerhardie's writing. Would you seek political information, moral instruction or even sociological analysis in a symphony? If not, then do not look for them here. The implications of such things may exist, but not the things themselves. From all those fashionable and transitory concerns that enable the literary historian neatly to 'place' an author in the ranks of literature Gerhardie seems remarkably free— temporarily, perhaps, to his loss. For his aim is to combine, not segregate. Therefore we must not look in his writing for one aspect of life divorced from another, we must not seek, in isolation, some specialist grain of undisolved information—on unemployment, for example, in the 1920s, or the machinery of the Spanish Civil War. About hunger and war we may read in Gerhardie's books, but not for their own sake, not treated as if they represented the whole of life. His purpose is to create works of beauty, and he sets out to achieve this by the tone of his writing, by keeping in equilibrium many feelings and attitudes that we tend to think of as incompatible—in particular what is actual with what we conceive to be ideal. He blends realism with romanticism, romanticism with irony. The skill lies in doing this in such a way that the romantic element does not make the story less real but more so, that the irony does not obliterate romance, for reality is all these things and even a lie is an aspect of the truth. It is in the orchestration of these diverse elements that Gerhardie excels. As with symphonic music, the delight derives not from guessing what is to come next, but from our memory of its design, from our delighted recognition of the cunning of its parts, our concurrence in the cumulative fitness of the whole. The ampersand is his cipher of a latitudian vision when all things stand revealed existing in their own right, resolved in paradise, announced in *This Present Breath* where there is no more *but*, and all is *and*, and all is green in that untravelled land.

Since explanation is death in fiction, we should not seek a 'message' in Gerhardie's books. He does not tell us what to think or how to be better citizens, nor does he instruct us who is wrong and who right in these stories. As with life itself we must come to our own conclusions, and enjoy them for the pleasure which they contain. In the story, for example, 'In the Wood', we do not know for certain whether Lieutenant Barahmeiev will make love to the landlord's wife. We do not know whether he is what he seems to be, an empty bluffer, or whether she is in part deceitful. We can read it several ways. The story carries within it another miniature Gerhardie short story in the Lieutenant's recollection of his inconclusive first love affair, and in his audience's response to this story we may hear a parody of the obtuse critic's reaction to Gerhardie's work, a warning of how not to read him.

> The Lieutenant ceased.
> 'Well?' we said. 'Go on.'
> 'That's all,' said the Lieutenant.
> 'But what happened afterwards?' asked Vera Solomonovna.
> 'Nothing happened.'
> 'But *how*?' she said in a tone as though she had been wronged.

'Well, that's all there is to tell.'

'But—it's no proper story even.'

'I can't help that,' he answered, almost angrily. 'This is what happened, and this is where it ended. I can't falsify the facts to suit your taste. We don't, my dear Vera Solomonovna, live our lives to provide plots for stories.'

Nor, conversely, should novelists write stories for those who simply want to escape from life. This is not to say that Gerhardie's stories are, as the Lieutenant's was thought to be, pointless or without a moral. 'A Bad End', the story of an unintentional act of manslaughter, the trial for murder, conviction and execution of Mr Proudfoot—accorded the seal of authenticity by Lord Birkenhead, a former Lord Chancellor—was used as propaganda against capital punishment by Victor Gollancz. 'The Vanity Bag', too, is susceptible to moral interpretation. The American who falls in love with a girl in Salzburg, whose vanity-bag must needs convince him in the end that he has nothing more to hope from her, is rewarded by the unsought heavy companionship of her literary father—a bag of vanity. But none of these stories are intended to provide us with answers to particular questions. They do not show us how life should be lived—they do not exhort us in this way. Instead they show us our ideals and illusions plus what is, in the material sense, reality. For life, as depicted by Gerhardie, is neither horrible nor happy, but strange and unique, transitory yet static, funny, beautiful and awful. 'But when one listens to music,' Chekhov wrote, 'all this is—that some people lie in their graves and sleep, and that one woman is alive and, grey-haired, is now sitting in a box in the theatre, seems quiet and majestic, and the avalanche [romantic love] no longer meaningless, since in nature everything has a meaning. And everything is forgiven, and it would be strange not to forgive.'

This simultaneous effect of life's diversity is the impression which Gerhardie's work creates, and when we read him we discover with delight that our half-realized thoughts concerning the fluidness, complexity and elusiveness of life have been articulately confirmed.

MICHAEL HOLROYD

TRISTAN UND ISOLDE

HE met her at one of those numerous little dancing clubs of Vienna which assemble regularly once a week at a particular café, where the facilities for introduction are only equalled by the ease of admission. When he asked where they could meet again, she told him, smiling sweetly, where to call her up next day, and he noticed that, besides having beautiful grey eyes with lashes like black needles and luxuriant black hair, she had an even, gapless semicircle of white teeth and, at the corners of her mouth, the foreshadowing of a moustache in after years. "And what name?"

"Ask for Fräulein Isolde."

"Isolde! How romantic! Will you dance?"

"I do not dance." She smiled divinely.

"Well, it's a relief, if anything. I am tired of jazz music, tired of having to prance about every night on my best feet on the dubious chance of meeting a nice girl."

"I like," she said, "to sit at home with a book."

9

" I can't tell you how glad, how——"

" Are you fond of Art ? "

" Love it ! "

" I will take you to the Art-Historical Museum."

" Good ! "

She closed the eyes with the long lashes and nodded rapidly in response. Her brows twitched. And he loved her.

Next day they met at a café in the Ring. She turned up three-quarters of an hour after the appointed time in a black coat, black hat, and a black frock buttoned to the neck. With dark abundant locks and pale powdered face she sat, mysterious, smoking innumerable cigarettes. And only asked, " What is it like in America ? "

" Very nice," he said.

" Are you studying here ? "

He nodded. She smoked on.

A dingy pock-marked poet came in and sat down beside them and opened the portfolio he carried stuffed with his writings. She laid a tender hand on his shoulder, scanning the while the pages of a story. " Yes," she commended. " You have hit it off all right."

They motored to the castle of Schönbrunn and sat

in a summer-house by the water, romantically, and walked in the park. He took her arm tenderly. She was sad. "Why?" he asked.

"Memories." They walked on in silence. "We shouldn't have come here," he said. She pressed his arm in mute recognition. He helped her into the motor. "You're so kind and tender to me. I am not used to it," she said. He kissed her hand in dumb adoration. "I woke up this morning and smiled. I wondered why I was smiling, and then remembered I had met a nice man."

"When I leave Vienna you must come abroad with me," he said jestingly.

"It's not out of the question," she answered seriously.

He talked glibly about the dearth of intellectual satisfactions. "You're so different from other girls. Your nature is artistic."

"I will show you round the gallery," she said.

When they went—"This is a picture over which I wept," she told him.

"This is not bad," he said, stopping at a Rembrandt.

"Yes, he has hit it off." Her eyes filled.

"What is it?"

" We used to come here, Hans and I."

" And where is he now ? "

" Dead."

" Long ? "

" Nine months.   We had been engaged three years. And then, suddenly, he died—for no reason—of a mere cold.   So young—twenty-two."

" But you too are so young, you have your life to live."

" It's all in the past."

" No, no !   And you're so beautiful."

" I will show you my big picture."

He waited in the motor while she ran upstairs to the apartment to fetch it.

" Wonderful ! " he commented.

" Now I must rush back, father is waiting.   And you can have the picture of me till we meet again to-morrow."

But she stepped inside and they went for another ride with the picture.   " Where to ? " asked the man.

" Round and round," she said.   She crossed her legs, the skirt slipping up above her knees, and lit a cigarette.   And suddenly he leaned over to her and kissed her on the mouth.

" Tut-tut-tut— You mustn't kiss. Wait till I kiss you."

" I *have* waited," he answered, " and I'm still waiting, and, by God! I can't wait any longer " (with the taximeter piling up, he thought, piling up all the time while we wait, and the chauffeur the only one to gain by it).

" This is the Prater," she said.

" Where to ? " asked the taxi-man.

" Round and round," he said dismally.

She burst out laughing. " You said this so funnily ! " She gave him a furtive kiss on the lips. " What is your name ? "

" I have a silly name. I'm called Ebenezer."

" It is—rather silly."

" Well, you needn't call me by it. You can invent another name for me."

She considered. " Peter," she said.

" All right—Peter."

When she fell ill he sent her flowers, and every day she sent a message—that she was a little better, or a little worse. Then she came again to the café. " Beautiful, beautiful flowers ! I was breathless when I saw them. And so much ! "

He buried his face in her hands, " Beautiful girl

. . . beautiful flowers. Wonderful when I think: I've been seeking, all these months, all these years I've been seeking, and now I have found."

"I too. For nine months I was alone. Now when I come to the café, the waiter says confidentially: 'The gentleman is already here.' One feels one has somebody."

"While you were ill, when I used to come here by myself, the waitress looked at me with sad eyes, as if she thought you'd left me or we had broken it off. I notice we've become privileged guests and are treated accordingly."

She smiled—so sweetly and intimately, and, watching him, laughed. He looked up from his cup. "I must laugh," she said, "at the way you scratch the last drop of sugar out of the cup." He laughed too. She was delightful. "I've just come back from Adolf's bedside," she remarked.

"And who is Adolf?"

"My fiancé."

"This is new to me."

"At least he thinks he is my fiancé."

"And you don't think so."

"No."

"This is a relief."

14

" He is dying now."

" Oh—is he ? " And secretly he thought : This is a relief. " What does he do ? "

" He is a doctor—venereal and skin diseases. But he is very tender and aesthetic and plays the piano wonderfully—Schumann and Chopin. He says he will let me live as I like and love whom I like, that he will never touch me, and only wants to be allowed to marry me and to live by my side."

When they came out of the café, it was a sunny afternoon. " Come, I'll show you where I live," he said, and they made their way to Am Hof—the old-fashioned square of Vienna where he had rooms. She took off her hat and used his comb and sat down at his writing-table. " It must be nice to live like that. If I were you I would give myself up to my work, and never tie myself up with any woman."

" How you understand me ! Other women are so conventional and self-seeking. But you—you are so delightfully free and easy, so unusual and romantic ! "

She sat in his chair, and suddenly sleep overcame her. " I want to lie down." She lay down on his bed, and he sat down beside her. " I feel like a faithful old dog sitting at your feet and seeing that you come to no harm." She gave him her hand, which he pressed to his lips. He looked at her legs in the glossy silk stockings, the seductive shoe. Warm, yielding curves, unexplored mysteries. And he said, " After all this seeking, to feel you have found . . . at last. It's not—no, not your face; it's . . ." He was gently pressing her knee; she made an involuntary attempt to disengage it. " . . . your soul," he said—and she left it. " I'm content: I really need nothing. Not by a word would I suggest or precipitate the moment. . . . Not till you yourself . . . an offering, a priceless gift." She pressed his hand to her heart. " Not even then. I'm content, I need nothing." She touched his brow silently with her lips.

" Yes ? " he asked, suddenly crushing her in his arms. " Yes ? "

She closed her eyes with the lashes like black needles, nodding rapidly several times. " Pull down the blinds."

" Oh, I am grateful ! Tristan and Isolde . . . *Nacht der Liebe* . . ." He was whistling.

" Is the door locked ? "

" I'll lock it for you—do anything for you."

Of sheer relief, he felt like cracking cheap jokes.

" What is the time ? "

"It's four o'clock in the afternoon—the time people here take their 5 o'clock tea." The yellow blinds drew to and fro in the breeze. Outside in the sunny square the women were selling oranges and flowers. Upstairs somebody began playing the piano. "This is Schumann," she said. "Adolf plays this." The blinds still swayed gently, gently, and they could feel the breeze on their burning cheeks. She knitted her brows. "What are you thinking?" he asked.

"Adolf is waiting for me. I've neglected supper for father."

He turned on the switch. "No, no, I am ashamed of the light."

It was black night when they went out. Stepping into the taxicab at the door, she gave her address. "You shouldn't have told him where you live before that old caretaker woman. You never can tell."

"I take full responsibility for what I do and I am prepared to face the consequences of my acts, and I have nothing to be ashamed of," she said. He remembered the prudish cowardly attitude of his own forget-me-not eyed sisters, his mother, his maidenly aunts. "You wonderful girl!" he exclaimed. He

17

felt grateful, so that he did not even mind how much he had to pay for the taxi. She scanned his face and his figure, and he instantly looked at his gloves. " They are filthy, I know."

" Give them to me, I will wash them for you."

" No, no, why should you ? "

" The maid will wash them."

" Very well, then."

The taxicab pulled up at her house door. " Just see me upstairs. It's so dark." She took hold of his arm and with a sure quick step ran up the stairs, while he fumbled uncertainly with his feet. She gave him a kiss in the dark, which missed the mark, handed him the house door key, begged him for the sake of love not to make a noise—and was gone. He felt his way carefully by the chalk wall, dirtying his coat and hands— and presently lost himself. For an hour he fumbled about in the dark, groping his way down the steps time without end, only to find himself at the end of each attempt in the coal cellar. Now I've made a noise, he thought, the caretaker will come out, call the police and have me arrested. I'm a lost man. When, having given up all hope, suddenly he saw a shimmering of light, then a new turning, the real stairs — and he was saved. The Votive

Church as he went home seemed made of lace: the tall twin towers, like a prayer, strained heavenward in the blue night. He sat down on a bench and thought of her.

He was more than usually courteous to the old caretaker woman. "A pretty girl, I call her," she said, opening the heavy outer door for him, while he paid the customary "lock-out money." "Is she your bride?"

He nodded.

"Ah, well, young men have luck. But I'm not one to let the cat out of the bag."

He fumbled in his pockets.

"Thank you.—I am known to be discreet. Baron Waldmeyer who lived here nine months ago also used to bring his bride up to his rooms, regularly three times a week you might say. A pretty girl she was, too, Lina Holz—you know the chemist's daughter across the way. The white house opposite. That's right. Never a word to anybody. God beware! They were very satisfied with me. 'Frau Krampf,' he used to say to me, 'I can rely on you.'"

Next day they were hurrying in the train into the country. "I too am glad we're friends," she said.

" My family is nothing to me. Mother died when I was fourteen. She was so small I used to take her on my lap. My sister married rich, but she can't do anything decently. She is such a snob—hides the fact that we are Jews. She will give father a new suit—or rather says she will—and all so haughtily, you know, so condescendingly, will talk so much about it and in the long run won't buy him anything and will even borrow money from him in the end. She gives me things occasionally, or rather says she will and doesn't. But that which is inside one she doesn't know."

" Quite."

Yet he had discovered that Isolde, despite her intellectual pretensions, was as fond of cabarets and dancing halls as any other child of pleasure-loving Vienna. And she was not content with going to one cabaret during a night, but from the one immediately wanted to go on to another, and from that to a third—in all respects similar to the first.

" I'm different," she said. " Already as a child we had no points of contact. My sister would go out on the Korso to be stared at by men, while I sought my friends among writers and artists, or went off by myself to the Opera and tried to find my real ' I ' in the

Walküre, the *Ring*, the *Meistersinger*, in *Tristan und Isolde*."

" Very becoming for one named Isolde ! If one didn't know you were above such cheap romanticism, one would almost suspect you gave yourself that name."

She laughed faintly.

" Why—*did* you ? "

She closed her eyes and nodded rapidly.

" How clever of you ! " He kissed her hand.

" My real name is Rebecca."

" Let's forget that it is. We'll go to the Opera together—to *Tristan*. A good performance here, isn't it ? "

She closed her eyes and nodded rapidly, significantly. " I'll bring the complete musical score. I have the entire *partitura* and we can follow it."

" By God ! we'll follow it ! " said he, though he was quite unable to read music.

At the Opera, all the liveried attendants seemed to know her. " Ah, Fräulein Isolde, it's good to see you again ! "

" It's the first time that I have been here since (her eyes filled)—his death." And she ushered him upstairs through draughty corridors with the air of a proprietress showing a visitor round the premises. " Here Hans and I used to sit. Or, when we had little money, we stood over there or sat on the steps."

" A fine Opera House."

" Yes, this is my temple."

She carried an enormous book—the complete musical score of the piece, and they sat down and he read the biographical note, while the orchestra enclosure gradually filled and the executants began tuning up their instruments.

" Because I have never known love in real life I want now to realize it in music." Thus Wagner one day wrote to Liszt. " I have jotted down in my head a *Tristan und Isolde*, the simplest but the most full-blooded of musical conceptions : with the black flag which flies at the end I then want to cover myself and to—die."

There was a meagre trickling of applause : the conductor threaded his way to his seat, passed his hand over the page under the green-shaded lamp, raised the *bâton*, and began. They sat close together, the Prelude with its high-stepping, long-striding sinuous tentacles groping after new resting-places, far out of reach, yet working out its salvation surely and steadily, swelling

22

and widening, till—the conductor shaking his locks
and his fists—the brass blared its compelling response ;
and, in a tide of regaining tranquillity, the Prelude
gradually evened itself out to the level at which it
began, and the curtains parted, revealing the ship.
She followed the score with a preoccupied air, now and
then nodding her head with that significant look of
critical recognition ; but when he asked for the place
they were at she never could find it and began turning
the pages backward and forward, six at a time and in
vain. And when, in the second act, King Marke's
hunting horns died away and the cast-down torch went
out, to a heart-sinking, intolerably dulcet cadence, and
the night was all astir, and Tristan staggered to Isolde,
and the great theatre plunged into the most passionately voluptuous music that has ever been, then they
pressed each other's fingers more tightly and their
nerves throbbed in unison—until King Marke, returning at a moment least desired from the hunt, surprised
the twain. In this passionate music, more truly voluptuous than the grosser senses of man can divine, there
lies concealed a certain pledge : a foretaste, maybe,
of a reality awaiting us, or one we needs must forgo,
wrenched from a far world by a genius, for us to partake
of before we go under.

In the interval he read more of the biography. Wagner, while working on *Siegfried*, wrote to a friend : " My musical sensibility already sways far beyond it— thither where my mood belongs : into the realm of melancholy." It was his love for Mathilde Wesendonck—a love of denial for both—which determined the work. " That I have written Tristan I thank you out of my deepest soul into all eternity." Thus he writes to her three years after completion. It has been said that the musical drama is unreal because the love in it is the artificial outcome of the love potion given to Tristan and Isolde during the voyage instead of the death drink they bargained for. But the potion, of course, is a symbol. Love was latent in them, but could not face the light of day : it is the belief in the certainty of their death held for them in the cup which works the love miracle. Only in death can they give each other. But of that " realm of stilled longings " they had been cheated. He was there—*Der öde Tag !* And now the third and last act—the empty sea, the hollow day, the dreary convalescence, with the black flag already flying over their destinies. They sat and listened to the sundown glow now sensible in the familiar bars of this greatest of love-tragedies—as it had always been.

The measured strains of the *Liebestod* had grown quicker and more passionate ; Isolde, wrenching her hands, was racing along with the orchestra, which, at this turn, was taking the melody from her, easily, in rapidly rising voluptuous strains, climbing, slipping, climbing anew, rapidly, rapidly, to a climax, now, now. . . . The conductor, forgetting his quasi-reticent attitude, rose in his seat and with a sweep of his stick commanding one hundred and twenty-six instruments, drowned her top notes in a mighty volume of rapturous sound.   But she did not mind.   Nor did anyone mind. On that plane of emotion one does not mind : one felt one wanted to go home, cover oneself with the black flag—and die. . . .

They made their way past the draughty swinging doors into the lighted streets and stood a while in the crowded Opernring, Peter taking her arm.   He was elated.   He tried to whistle bits he remembered, but she stopped him with a frown.   In the café she seemed moody and irritable.   " *Must* you always scratch the cup out ? "

" I feel I am wasting my life if I don't."

" Why don't you lick it out with your tongue ? "

" What is the matter ? "

" I must talk to you very seriously."

" Well ? "

" Another day—to-morrow."

He would have died of anxiety if he had to wait till to-morrow. " To-night or not at all."

" About our—relation. I want to have it out with you. I don't want you to be merely playing with me and then, when it suits you, drop me." They were going down the teeming Kärntnerstrasse and bent their way into the Graben, walking up the famous Korso. " Here is father's jeweller's shop."

" What's all this nonsense ? " he asked peremptorily.

" Father's been bullying me. No money to give me. Business going to ruin. No one buying jewellery nowadays. ' *Ein Skandal !* You're twenty-two and I, a man of eighty-six, have to go on supporting you ! ' and so on, and so forth. My brother-in-law sits and talks to my father and tells him I ought to get married. And father curses me : ' Again you've been out all night. A good bride and no mistake, Adolf sitting and waiting for you here all the evening ! ' Of course, he is right in a way. But I never promised definitely to Adolf. I tell him, ' Adolf, I value your feeling for me, and if no one better crops up I will marry you in the end.' So he sits in our drawing-room all evening

26

after leaving the venereal disease hospital, waiting for me and playing Chopin."

Peter thought of what he might say, but couldn't say much. " Damn him ! " he said.

" And I mean—I don't want to be playing ducks and drakes with Adolf, who is a man of fine feeling—"

" But hasn't he died ? He was going to."

" He wasn't a bit. He only put himself to bed so as to get me to come and sit at his bedside and hold his hand. And what I mean is, a man has a love affair, then another, a third, a fourth, and is only looked up to, even by women. But a girl has to think."

" Is there — is there — well, you know what I mean ? "

" No, there isn't. All the same——"

" But why say it like that ? "

" You should have thought of saying it yourself. I waited long enough."

" But why in the world did you make out you were unconventional—romantic—God knows what—unlike other women ? Why did you ? "

" I thought you expected it."

Damned shameless lie, he thought ; and said aloud :

"This would not appear to correspond with the facts. Secretly you were out for marriage from the start and only pretended — don't I see it now!—but all the time you were on the hunt for a husband."

"You needn't flatter yourself. I'm good-looking enough to marry any time I want to. And such birds as you I can find on every bush."

"Thank you."

They had reached her house. "Well, am I to ring you up to-morrow as usual?" Her voice was not friendly.

"As usual," he said, and thought: As per usual, business as usual. But the irony of using such decrepit war slang would be lost on her. That was the worst of it all: they hadn't really many points of contact. And making the most of the few they had, he pressed forward to kiss her.

"No."

He shrugged his shoulders, raised his hat and went. He went by the familiar Kolowratring that he had paced no end of times before—in other, happier days. How far away they seemed now!

Next day at two she did not call him up. At three she had not called him up. By five his anxiety had reached seething point. She would not call him up. She would never call him up. He was lost—damned. In all Vienna he could not find a place for himself. He sat and waited, hoping, doubting. And then, together with her friends, she came, as if not noticing him, and was about to sit down at a table, when he went after her and spoke. She turned round, abashed. " You are deadly pale," he said. " Are you frightened, or what ? "

" No. But I didn't expect to meet you here."

" And I waited—five hours. God, how I suffered ! "

She looked round at him to see if it was true. His face was haggard. She was not unkind to him, yet took little notice of him, only now and then, after the performance of an item turning to him with a—" Quite good, wasn't it ? "

" Very good ! " He was happy—come what might —for the abating of his erewhile suffering. He begged for an appointment next day and obtained one, and they lunched together at a freshly-painted table of the restaurant in the Volksgarten. The foliage was bursting out and everywhere along the Ring the cafés were putting out their little " gardens." He glanced at her legs in the flesh-coloured stockings. How romantically realistic—as if straight from Maupassant!

he thought.   And took her hand.   She withdrew it.
He took it again.   " Don't touch me."

" Why not ? "

" I can't."

He remembered a cabaret singer in Vienna who sang
in a feeble hoarse voice : " I can't, I can't, I'm weak
on the chest," and then immediately after in a voice
that would put brass trumpets to shame, a voice so
powerful that it made the window panes rattle—" I
CAN'T, I CAN'T, I'M WEAK ON THE CHEST ! ! ! "
And he asked, " What do you mean ' I can't ' ?   You're
not weak on the chest ? "

She did not laugh.   " Something has broken within
me—and I don't know if it can ever be put right."

" Then we must set about mending it."

" There is a gulf, the bridge has been broken.
I can never come back.   I can't help it.   I've lost all
feeling for you."

" But, my darling, we're mending it, aren't we ? "

" It can never be mended."

How charmingly she walked, with feet a little outward and swaying slightly from the hips.   There was
something of the awkward school girl about her.
Would she ever come back ?

But one day, as the scent of jasmine hovered in the

air and he gently passed his hand over her own and said, " My love, come back to me," she closed her eyes with the lashes like black needles and nodded rapidly.

The bridge was mended.

His emotion of gratitude ran to kissing. " Can't you sit still ? " she admonished him.

" But you are mine. Don't you want to be ? "

" Not in that way." *Her* love ran to emotion.

" In that way. Or I feel I am wasting my time."

" Ach ! " she waved him aside like a fly. Then angrily, wearily : " Pull down the blinds ! " She began to unhook her high collar at the neck. " Is the door locked at least ? "

He smiled reassuringly. " I've taken requisite steps against the possibility of King Marke appearing when he is least wanted."

He held her in his arms, and sang : " You Tristan, I Isolde, no more Tristan ! . . ."

" Shut up ! "

" There is little poetry in you."

" And you are a beast."

" Thank you." And looking at her, drinking her in with his eyes, he thought, " Poor Richard Wagner ! Who had never known such love as this ! "

He thought so. He thought so a long time, when

she attracted his attention. " What do you want
to do ? "

" Go home."

" No-o."

" No-o ! " she mimicked him angrily. " You're
like that—never enough of a good thing—lick the sugar
out of the bottom of the cup when there's nothing
left."

" Ha-ha ! "

" Nothing to laugh at."

He sang : " *Der öde Tag !* "

He went to the adjoining room. When he returned
she had her coat on and was powdering her face before
the mirror. As they were leaving, " Put the light out,"
she said. At the café she read the paper and hardly
spoke to him. He looked at his associate in sin. Her
face was still beautiful. Sin sat lightly upon her.
He remembered afterward how they sat in the taxicab
—how it rained outside. She only said, " Oh, yes,
I've still got your gloves. You will get them to-
morrow." At the gate she gave him her hand, looked
into his eyes, very kindly, he noticed, and said—
" Peter, farewell."

" Good-bye. Matches ! " he cried after her.

" Don't want any."

Walking home, he remembered her words and the strangeness of the " farewell " dawned upon him. Returning, he found a note on the table which he had not perceived as they went out. On the back of a slip " Rimless Stockings. Best Quality " he read : " We shall never see each other again. I *cannot*.— Isolde."

And then came a letter.

" Peter, I have not much to tell you, but I have the feeling that you are still waiting for something. Somehow a cleft has arisen between us, which can never be bridged. Is it the fulfilment in us, was this giving one's self also the end ? I do not know, but it may well be so.

" In me there is no mourning, not a shimmer of disappointment, no reproach either for you or for me. And now I know why so long I could not find any words for you.

" And so farewell, Peter, I wish you the best of luck in all the coming years.

ISOLDE."

It was Easter. He strolled about by himself. When he perceived a black hat and flesh-coloured stockings, he invariably thought it was she. And the town was setting itself for the spring; the gardens, the freshly painted tables and chairs beckoned invitingly. He remembered how he had felt lost and damned when she had not telephoned to him one day, and now felt doubly lost—doubly damned. What sort of thing was life? What sort of creature was man? Daunted by tiny reverses, already squirming like a worm at a woman's feet. There he was, just like Adolf, he who had been so sure of himself, supplicating for mercy, begging her for a morsel of bread. He strolled all alone about the town, waited at her gate, sat in the garden where (he remembered her telling him, though it had scarcely interested him at the time) she had played as a child. There were rows of seats lined with mothers and nurses. A little boy in the park was kicking a ball. A nice little fellow, he thought, but he'll probably grow up to be a blackguard. Suddenly he saw her sitting with her friends. A hot pang shot through his heart. She spoke to him pleasantly but dispassionately. " How are you, Peter? How is life treating you? "

" Rottenly."

When he had a chance to speak to her alone he supplicated for an interview.

" Child, it's no use," she said wearily.

" Yes, yes, a quarter of an hour—eye to eye—to discuss matters—to talk things over."

" All right then, to-night at 8.30."

When they did meet—at 9.30—he found that he had nothing to discuss, nothing to talk over. He only wanted her, craved for her physical beauty with all the strength of his physical being. She knew a subtler passion that hovered in her breast and was more like music, that went out in long curves and found no resting-places. And to her he had been part of that elusive dream. " Forgive me, Isolde, but really it's your fault. You put it all so clumsily. Marriage. Yes. Even so, what can I do now ? "

At the word marriage her eyes lit up and a smile played on her face.

" What can I say now ? I can't say : Isolde, marry me. I perfectly understand you can't say—your pride won't allow you to say, yes."

" I'll go back to my memories. I knew I should have to be alone. I will never have another like Hans."

" I know it's the bitter lot of those to follow him to fare badly by comparison. Alas ! no live virtue stands the ghost of a chance at the side of retrospective illusion."

She looked at him sharply. " The comparison does not arise. I didn't *love* you."

" But then why, may I ask—yes, precisely, why— ? "

" Because I thought you expected it."

" Look here. Listen. I want to tell you something."

" Better hold your tongue."

" I expect——" it was a desperate step—" yes, I expect you to marry me."

Her face lit up at the word. She played with the idea. " I don't deny "—she puffed at a cigarette— " that it would have certain immediate advantages. Father was carrying on again this morning. '*Ein Skandal !* I, an old man with one foot in the grave, have to keep you.' ' What do you want me to do ? ' I cried at last. ' You never taught me a thing. All the shops and offices are reducing their staff. Do you want me to go on the streets ? ' He slapped my face. I went to my room and cried. Later he came to me. He was sorry. ' I'd like to see you settled before I close my eyes.' He'd be glad, and I'd be glad to make him happy. Let me see, I'd have a little money if I married—not much, still a trifle."

" Who from ? "

" My brother-in-law promised. Then there are

silver things—knives and forks, solid silver—not much, but still something."

Der öde Tag !

"Father might be prevailed upon to give something from his shop. Then furniture—a bedstead—two chairs. My sister has taken the mattress, though it didn't belong to her. My mother left it to me."

The vulgarity of it—things—cupboards—carpets—meddling relations. How dismal was our human fate ! He felt that one had but to set one's ship towards romance, to realise how fruitless were one's hopes and how soon frustrated ! She thought of her father, of the end of squalor and deceit, the joy of her brother-in-law, her own home, children, wealth. "But—" she scarcely meant it—" but I can't. It's not honest towards you for me to accept a solution for reasons of convenience only."

"So you can't ? " He was almost relieved.

"I can't."

All the misery and anguish of his loneliness, his intolerable loneliness dawned upon him. He had spent a week without her. He knew what it was like. "Come, it really looks as though you didn't want to make me happy for my own sake !"

" Well, if you are sure that it will make you happy."

He was not sure. (He was sure of the contrary.) He drank his cup to the bottom and then took the spoon and licked off the sugar, while she watched him critically. And he thought : She won't let me drink my coffee as I like. She won't let me do anything as I like. I'm a lost man.

She said, " We must look at it sensibly. We both will have our advantages. You will be proud of showing me to your people and friends, while I shall be doing things for you at home." He looked at her : she was too small and when she walked she waddled like a duck. Indeed, what would his sisters think of it ? He pictured her at forty, at fifty, sixty and seventy, while he pictured himself all the while at twenty-five. She complained a good deal of her father, but if the old man found fault with her it was, of course, with good cause. " I'll mend this for you," she would say—and never did. " I must visit Hans's grave to-morrow "— but she went to a dance instead. He recalled that she had not yet returned his gloves—after keeping them two months !

" But why are you looking so wretchedly sad ? I've not accepted you yet."

" Not a bit." He imagined his arrival with his dark bride in the United States, their appearing before his proud " one hundred per cent. American " mother, the astonishment of his slim forget-me-not eyed sisters, the curve of their raised brows.

" If I married—" and she looked at him out of the corner of the eye to see how he took it, " we'd have separate bedrooms."

He smiled faintly. It was past a joke.

" Cheer up. You look as though somebody has done you out of your money. I can see it won't do. You're so cold, so calculating, so concentrated on yourself. I am sure I could never marry you. I was merely joking."

" No joke, I meant it. It's settled—you're my bride and I'm your blooming bridegroom."

" Your first experience ? "

" Yes. I feel like a fool."

" Thank you," she smiled. " It's my second." She looked at her hands. " May I keep Hans's ring ? "

" Yes," he said gloomily. Hans. Fritz. Grete. Nauseating relations. They'll want to congratulate him, see the ring, touch it, maybe—all the dark Jewish brood, dentists, skin-disease doctors, stock-exchange frequenters. A nosing father—perhaps suggesting purchasing the engagement ring at his own shop, offering a wedding ring " cheap " in advance, or questioning the value of it if bought elsewhere—belittling the outlay—pooh-poohing expense. It was unbearable.

" Do your people speak German ? "

He shook his head abjectly.

" Then you must teach me English.'

" I'll try." He pictured her dumbness, her being tied to him night and day, his mother and sisters asking her easy simple questions : " How—do—you —like—America ? " and her asking back : " Please ? " every time. A bewildered aunt of his struggling with a dictionary to make herself understood. Isolde smiling propitiatorily at his mother, trying to curry favour with her, to appear the tender wife ; and he the heavy father to their common children.

" You needn't look so unhappy. I haven't accepted you yet."

" It's one o'clock, the café's closing," he said peremptorily, and called to the waiter : " *Herr Ober !* *Zahlen !*—Yes or no ? "

She did not answer, but smiled shyly. He took an empty cigarette box, unscrewed his fountain-pen, and wrote :

" ? "

She took the fountain-pen from him and wrote :
" 1 "

He quibbled : " Is that an affirmative or perhaps an equally determined negative ? "

She did not answer. He helped her on with her coat and while he was putting on his own, slowly, pensively she was collecting her things into the bag : the powder-puff, the lip stick, the remaining cigarettes. He watched her eagerly. If she took the cigarette box with his " ? " and her " 1 " it meant—he knew what it meant. It meant that in after years she would be saying : " On this empty cigarette box my husband once proposed marriage to me." She would say it, a grey-haired gouty old woman, with a deep black moustache and a beard, lying in bed with one complaint or another, in a cap, her teeth in the glass at her side. She would say it to their children, little hairy black Jews creeping about everywhere : to her children's children ; and all those long years he'd be tied to her. Her gaze lingered on the cigarette box, and her thoughts from this chance *memento* of a romantic proposal swayed to that which it meant, her new life in America, her newly-gained freedom, the long-awaited salvation. But she noticed his searching critical look and did not take the *memento*.

" Yes or no, for the last time ? "

They were moving to the door into the street, where the rain was beginning to dribble, and stood still on the pavement.

She shook her head, and he made a movement to go. She wanted him to say something to hold him back. " Here are your—your gloves, Peter." And tears seemed to come to her eyes.

He took them as a sign, pressed her hand and went his way hurriedly. At the corner a gust of wind blew the rain against his face and tried for his hat. He did not know what he had done, why he had done it, or what had been done to him. He only knew he wanted to go home, cover himself with the black flag—and die.

THE BIG DRUM

THE brass band played *Im Köpfle zwei Äugle*, and it seemed to her that the souls of these men were like notes of this music, crying for something elusive, for something in vain. To blare forth one's love on a brass trumpet! An earnest of one's high endeavour fallen short through the inadequate matter of brass; but withal in these abortive notes one felt the presence of the heights the instrument would reach, alas, if it but could!

It touched her to the heart. She would have liked her Otto to play the trumpet instead of the big drum. It seemed more romantic. Otto was not a bit romantic. He was a soldier all right, but he looked more like a man who started life as a shoemaker's apprentice, had grown old and was still a shoemaker's apprentice. The band played well—a compact synthetic body— but Otto was a forlorn figure who watched the proceedings with sustained and patient interest and was suffered by them, every now and then to raise his drumstick and to give a solitary, judicious "Bang!"

And he—a tall gaunt man—seemed as though he was ashamed of his small part. And as she watched him she felt a pang of pity for herself; wedded to him, she would be forgotten, while life, indifferent, strode by; and no one in the world would care whether she had her share of happiness before she died. And the music brought this out acutely, as if along the hard stone-paved indifference of life it dragged, dragged on excruciatingly its living bleeding soul. It spoke of loneliness, of laughter, of the pathos, pity and futility of life.

She watched them. The bayonets at their side. The military badges of rank. The hard discipline. And the music seemed to say, " Stop ! What are you doing ? Why are you doing this ? " And thoughts flowed into her mind. Of soldiers dreaming on a Sunday afternoon. A fierce old corporal, of whom everyone was afraid, talking to her of children and of daisies. Soldiers who, too, had dreams in long waves—of what ? she did not know—but not this. And the men who stood up and blew the brass trumpets seemed to say, and the shining trumpets themselves seemed to say : " We were not born for the army : we were born for something better—though Heaven only knows what it is ! "

44

That was so. Undeniably so. Yet she wished it were otherwise. It helped to make allowances for Otto. Whatever else he lacked, it made her think at least he had a soul. But to be wedded for life to the big drum! She did not fancy the idea. It didn't seem a proper career. But Otto showed no signs of wanting to "get on"—even in the orchestra. The most exasperating thing about it all was that Otto showed no signs of even *trying!* She had asked him if he would not, in time, "move on" and take over —say, the double-bass. He did not seem to think it either feasible or necessary. Or *necessary!* He had been with the big drum for close on twelve years. "It's a good drum," he had said. And that was all.

There was no ... "go" in him. That was it: no go. It was no use denying it. As she watched him—gaunt and spectacled—she wished Otto were more of a man and less of an old maid. The conductor, a boozer with a fat red face full of pimples, some dead and dried up, others still flourishing, was a gallant —every inch a man. He had the elasticity and supple-ness and military alertness of the continental military man. She could not tell his rank from the stripes on his sleeves, but thought he must be a major. His heels were high and tipped with india rubber, and

so were straight and smart, but his trousers
lacked the footstrap to keep them in position—poor
dilapidated Austrian Army! How low it had sunk!
Nevertheless they were tight and narrow and showed
off the major's calves to advantage. He wore a pince-nez,
but a rimless kind, through which gazed a pair of
not altogether innocent eyes. But a man and a leader
of men. While Otto had no rubber on his heels.
His heels looked eaten away. He wore a pair of
spectacles through which he peered from afar at
his neighbour's music-stand, and at the appointed
time—not one tenth of a second too late or too early
—down came the drumstick with the long-awaited
" bang ! " So incidental, so contemptible was Otto's
part that, in addition to handling the drum, he had to
turn the pages for the man who played the cymbals.
It seemed to her humiliating. It was very wrong that
Otto had no music stand of his own.

He smiled shyly, and she turned away, annoyed.
The little modiste walked on, meeting the stream of
people who promenaded the path surrounding the
bandstand : a man on high heels, three girls with a
pinched look, a famous Tyrolese basso with a long
ruddy beard, a *jeune premier* with whiskers and hair
like a wig, whose look appeared to imply : " Here

46

am I." Innsbruck looked morose that Sunday morning and the military band in the park executed music that was tattered, gross, a little common, yet compelling, even like the daily fare of life. Oh, why were there no heroes? Of course she would have loved to be dominated. That's what men were for. She was a womanly woman. From Vienna. Exalted, brimming over with life. These men of the Tyrol! And as for Otto? Why, she could have only waved her hand!

She began to wonder whether she had not really better break it off with him. If men would but realise how little was required from them. Only an outward gesture of romance: a touch sufficed, the rest would be supplied by woman's powerful imagination. Not even so much. A mere abstention from the cruder forms of clumsiness, a surface effort to conceal one's feeblest worst. A mere semblance of mastery, a glimpse of a will. In short, anything at all that would provide the least excuse for loving him as she so wished to do. A minute she stood thinking. "A minimum. Hardly as much." There passed along the man on high heels, the three girls with the pinched look, the Tyrolese basso with the long ruddy beard, the *jeune premier* with whiskers and hair like a wig, whose look seemed to say, "Here am I"; then again the man on the high

47

heels, the three girls with the pinched look, the Tyrolese singer, and again the *jeune premier* whose look implied, "Here am I." They walked round and round as if the park were a cage and there was nothing to do but walk around—with heads bent, lifeless, sullenly resolute. And again there came along the man on high heels. "The minimum of a minimum...."

The music resumed. She consulted her programme. Item 7. Potpourri from the operette *Die Fledermaus* by Johann Strauss. She returned to the stand, prepared to give her fiancé another chance. Otto's part, as before, was contemptible, more contemptible than before. He was inactive. He smiled shyly. She coloured. And, looking at him, she knew. She knew it was no use, her love could not bridge the chasm. He was despised by the rest of the band. A stick-in-the-mud. Not a man. A poor fish. Not for her....

The potpourri, as if suddenly turning the corner, broke out into a resounding march, and behold, the big drum now led the way. Bang! bang! bang! bang! Clearly he whacked, never once missing the chance ; and the man with the cymbals, as if one heart and brain operated their limbs, clashed the cymbals in astounding unison, the big drum pounding away, pounding away, without cease or respite. And the trumpeters smiled, as who might say : " Good old big drum ! You have come into your own at last ! " Bang ! bang ! bang ! bang ! The big drum had got loud and excited. And all the people standing around looked as though a great joy had come into their lives ; and if they had not been a little shy of each other they would have set out and marched in step with the music, taken up *any* cause and, if only because the music implied that all men were brothers, gone forth if need be and butchered another body of brothers, to the tearing, gladdening strains of the march (since it is not known from what rational cause men could have marched to the war). And if in the park of the neighbouring town there was just such a band with just such a drum which played this same music, the people of the neighbouring town would have marched to this music and exterminated this town. The conductor, like a driver who, having urged his horse over the hill, leans back and leaves the rest to the horse, conceded the enterprise to the drummer, as if the hard, intricate work were now over and he was taking it easy ; his baton moved perfunctorily in the wake of the drum, he looked round and acknowledged the greetings of friends with gay, informal salutes of the left hand, his bland smile freely admitting to all that it was no longer himself but the

49

drum which led them to victory. Or rather, the hard fight had already been won and these, behold, were the happy results! Bang! bang! bang! bang! Strangers passed smiles of intimate recognition, old men nodded reminiscently, small boys gazed with rapt eyes, women looked sweet and bright-eyed, ready to oblige with a kiss; while the big drum, conscious of his splendid initiative, pounded away without cease or respite.

"Wonderful! Beautiful!" said the public surrounding them. And thought:

"Noise is a good thing."

The band had described the first circle and was repeating it with added gusto and deliberation. The drum and the cymbals were pounding, pounding their due through the wholly inadequate blazing of brass. But these did not mind: "Every dog has his day" —and they followed the lead of the drum. He led them. He—Otto! Her Otto was leading them. God! Merciful Virgin! What had she done to deserve such happiness? Otto! . . . And she had doubted him, thought there was no "go" in him. No *go!* She burnt red with shame at the mere thought of it. He was all "go." And didn't he make them go too, the whole lot of them? How he led them! Puffing, the sweat streaming down their purple faces, they blazed away till their cheeks seemed ready to burst, but Otto outdrummed them—annihilated their efforts. He—Otto ! O God ! Watching him, people could hardly keep still. But that none of them stirred and all of them wanted to, added piquancy to the illusion of motion. They stood rooted—while the drum carried on for them : Bang ! bang ! bang ! bang !

" Marvellous ! " sighed the public around them.

Her Otto—cock of the walk ! She could scarcely believe her eyes. Standing in front of the crowd, only a few paces from his side and raising herself on her toes ever so gently in rhythm with the music, so that by the very tininess of her movements she seemed to be sending added impetus into the band, as if, indeed, she were pressing with her little feet some invisible pump, she scanned his face with tenderness, in dumb adoration. And Otto at the drum must have felt it, for, at this turn, he put new life into his thundering whacks : *Bang ! bang ! bang ! bang !* he toiled, and the conductor, as if divining what was afoot, at that moment accelerated the pace of the march.

" Bravo, bravo ! " said the people surrounding them.

There was no doubt about it. This was Art. The unerring precision. The wonderful touch. Otto ! . . .

Otto, as never before, whacked the big drum, whacked it in excitement, in a frenzy, in transcending exaltation. Thundering bangs ! And now she knew—what she couldn't have dreamed—she knew it by his face. Otto was a hero. A leader of men. Something fluttered in her breast, as though a bird had flown in, ready to fly out.

" Now it's all over," thought the people, " and we are going home to lunch." And everyone smiled and felt very happy and gay. A sort of prolonged accelerated thundering of the big drum, and then one tremendous BANG !

The thing was over. The conductor raised a bent hand to the peak of his cap, acknowledging the applause. The bird in her fluttered more wildly than ever. She wanted to cry out, but her throat would not obey. She clutched at her heaving breast with trembling fingers. " My love," she thought. " My king ! My captain !——"

&

A BAD END

" Vengeance is mine, saith the Lord ; and that
means that it is not the Lord Chief Justice's."
Bernard Shaw.

Iᴛ all began by their talking of love and hate, as they
set out on a Sunday afternoon excursion to the moors.
Mr. Proudfoot advocated love and forgiveness;
Weaver maintained his faith in a good man's hate.
And Proudfoot hated Weaver and could not forgive
him because Weaver would not love and forgive.
On the way to the tramcar terminus Mr. Proudfoot
called in at the grocer's (it was Sunday, but the shop
was surreptitiously open, and Betty, the twelve-year-
old girl of the grocer, was reading assiduously a
threepenny novelette, entitled—he strained forward
to look—*Only a Mill Girl*). Having bought his usual
cigarettes, " Get away with you ! " rejoined Mr.
Proudfoot, continuing the argument.

" Undoubtedly ! " said Weaver stubbornly. He

envied the other his command of the pen, but doubted
if the author knew "life" as well as he, Weaver,
knew it. "*I* could give you material enough to fill
a dozen novels if you asked me," he would say, and
tell him of a thirty-stone man eating enough for three;
of a hangman in the neighbourhood who in his off-
duty hours was an innkeeper. "I want you to meet
him. A character for you. Bites off the heads of live
rats if a customer will stand beer all round." Mr.
Weaver was a dentist. There was something provo-
cative about all the dentists of Mr. Proudfoot's experience. They all pretended to ambitions outside their
profession. They had all wished to be writers, artists,
poets, composers or statesmen, and now handled their
surgical tools, extracted teeth, with a kind of embittered
"*Tant pis !*" The very first day on which Mr.
Proudfoot had called on Mr. Weaver in Gilbert Street,
Pedlar-with-Thresham, and inquired if it hurt to have
a tooth out, Weaver had said, "No. A second, and
it's out," and holding it between his pincers (while
his client rinsed his mouth with warm water and spat
out blood), the dentist was already discoursing: "Now
I've been reading about this Einstein fellow, you know,
and I've me own ideas about this 'ere relativity business,
if you know what I mean. I look at meself in the glass,

metaphorically, don't you know. But it does not follow, cosmically speaking like, that I present the same satisfactory appearance. In the same way, following the deductions of my—he, he—rather cynical philosophy, you'll think, flies, I say, may be as trivial and at the same time as important units in the cosmos as ourselves, and in the end their souls go back to the world-soul from which they sprang. Open your mouth."

" Is there a world-soul ? "

" *Undoubtedly !* " A rotund little body, smartly arrayed, Mr. Weaver went on : " This afternoon was a bit slack. Lately I haven't been feeling very well. And middle age is upon me. I thought of my past achievements. I had a look at my old medals—the one I got as a lad for swimming a race, and that other one for cycling, don't you know, and those other two for amateur boxing. My mother, ay, she was proud of 'em ! There." He sprinkled them out of a tin box on to his palm. " And I thought—how shall I say ? it didn't somehow seem as if it was ' enough,' if you know what I mean. Come, open your mouth."

" You're a cheerful old pessimist, aren't you ? " said Mr. Proudfoot, and opened his mouth.

" A cheerful pessimist ? That's what I call a contradiction in terms."

Mr. Proudfoot smiled, and thought (because he could not speak) that Weaver was rather like a man who, having grasped with difficulty the four simple rules of arithmetic, is bewildered at being told that he can waive them utterly in Algebra. He was fond of using difficult words unnecessarily, and would trot out a *cliché* on the slightest pretext. Mr. Proudfoot might say that he preferred horses to motor-cars, only to hear Weaver ejaculate : " A horse ! a horse ! my kingdom for a horse ! " Or Mr. Proudfoot might say that he had served in the cavalry during the war, for Weaver to remark, with lingering relish, " *Cavalleria Rusticana*." Or Mr. Proudfoot, perhaps in reference to the heavy rain, had only to let fall the word " deluge " for Weaver to comment : *"Après nous de déluge*, what ?" looking at him with a self-complacent smile, to see if he had noticed his culture. " I had a Frenchy here as an assistant once, but had to kick him out : his gift of the gab was too much for me. But I've picked up things, and I think I've got the hang of the lingo all right, what ? " But they had at once become friends, and in the evening Weaver would invite him to his house, push out his wife—a thin complacent

woman with a long aquiline nose which Weaver
thought aristocratic, and whose contribution to any
conversation did not extend beyond the invariable
affirmative: "That's right." "Out you go," he
would say, "we're an old bachelor party to-night.
—Now then," rubbing his hands. "Now for it! I've
been reading about this 'ere fellow Spinoza, you
know."

And so on till after midnight. Mr. Proudfoot
remembered these nights afterwards: Weaver, tottering
slightly after the beer, coming out into the open and
standing hatless in the middle of the street and saying
(in reply to Mr. Proudfoot desirous of making a
professional appointment with him on the morrow),
"Any day, old chap! any day!"

Arguing, they had reached the tram-car terminus
and boarded the train which was to take them on their
picnic out on to the moors. The world seemed trans-
figured that wet but happy afternoon. It seemed to
Mr. Proudfoot that everything was certainly for
the best in this best of all possible worlds. The
tram-cars were running smoothly and efficiently. The
gay, handsome conductor performed his duty as if it
were a pleasure. The policemen looked well fed, well
paid, well satisfied. Even the rain fell satisfactorily

from a dull but sober sky, and everybody was duly provided either with raincoat or umbrella—all was undoubtedly just as it should be. The world was well oiled and ran smoothly; everything was a wheel turning round easily on its axle, and God the Mechanic walked about his machinery and was well pleased.

And Mr. Proudfoot stood at once right inside and outside this astonishing world. He had a pointed beard, long hands, and a shy manner. His name was said to have been " Proudbottom." There is a theory that an ancestor of his applied for royal permission to annul the unpalatable name, and the Sovereign had been graciously pleased to amend the " bottom " to " foot." Now Weaver had felt from the first that Mr. Proudfoot was " different." And he was right. Mr. Proudfoot was an author of standing. And as for his being immortal, who can tell ? He wrote private letters with an eye to their posthumous publication, keeping a copy of each, in case his friends should lose or mislay them. He was a student of the old giants of literature, and he walked in their wake. He did not throw away his old sponge, for example, recalling that Goethe's was on exhibition at his famous house in Weimar, and accordingly gave his own to his sister to put away. As for the critics, whenever Mr. Proudfoot published a new book, they wrote: " Very suggestive...never a dull page... the interest sustained to the end. Nevertheless, one wishes that the author would break new ground, express life from a new angle...." But if he did leap over the fence and explore new tracks, " Go back, go back," they wrote in the newspapers, " get you back to the simple delights of your earlier books and we will listen to you till the crack of doom...." Mr. Proudfoot had arrived four months earlier in Pedlar-with-Thresham. And why, in God's name? you will ask. And indeed it would be difficult to imagine why anyone should arrive there, if he were not cursed by having to be there from the beginning. At the last General Election a local magnate in welcoming the Liberal candidate to Pedlar-with-Thresham from the dais raised outside the town hall, exclaimed with patriotic emotion: " In Pedlar-with-Thresham we spin well and vote well ! "

" Ay—and starve well ! " came a voice from the audience.

Such a place was Pedlar-with-Thresham. Mr. Proudfoot went there to get " local colour " for a Lancashire novel he was then writing. Nor was this the only reason. He had read in the newspapers of the low death-rate of Pedlar-with-Thresham and so, as he was afraid of dying young, he went to live there.

The sun had come out as the two men walked up on to the moors, arguing heatedly till Weaver, still maintaining his belief in hate, suggested good-naturedly, " Let's sit down here and have a go at what we've brought with us, what ? Open that basket. Come on, look out what you're doing ! See, you can't handle your tools properly. Oh my ! Watch me. That reminds me. I once captained a working men's football team up North, and had to take the blighters to London, where they were being entertained—mighty lavishly too ! They were the scum of the earth—no idea how to hold a tool or to behave in decent society. So I said to them ' Look here, you old blokes, watch me in everything, do just as I do, follow me, see ? and you'll be all right.' And I took the serviette—or what you fellows would call the table-napkin, I s'pose— placed it carefully on me seat and sat down on it. And they all—the whole blinking crew of 'em—got up, you know, placed their serviettes on their seats care- fully and sat down on 'em. Makes me roar even now when I think of it. Have another beer. Look here, old chap, shall we run up and see the hangman I told you about who bites off the heads of live rats—eh? He has his inn down the road further up on the moors. Good material for you, what?"

"I wouldn't go near one."

"Why? he's a necessary institution."

"I question that. If it is impossible to prevent homicidal maniacs from killing their fellows, then by all means let them forfeit their lives painlessly at the hands of a doctor. So much mercy is shown to mad dogs."

"You need a hangman to frighten folks with."

"Get away with you!"

"Undoubtedly!" said Weaver passionately.

"Nonsense. It's suffering to no purpose."

"It contributes in a way to the experience of the world-soul," said Weaver philosophically.

"Damn your world-soul! Damn your fanatical readiness to sacrifice real suffering units for the sake of God knows what misty and unfeeling generalities. You'll burn human beings in furnaces as sacrifices for what-not tin gods. You'll plunge into war for what-not shaky nationalist, imperialist, religious ideals. This fanatical *laisser faire*, this haplesss surrender of the only vital feeling thing—individual human life—for an abstraction ! It's just here that you let in Beelzebub, in the name of what-not vague and void resplendence ! "

"But there are compensations. Think of the pleasure a condemned man enjoys in knowing that the entire world is talking of him. They enjoy the vanity of it without a doubt."

" Get away with you ! "

" *Undoubtedly !* " said Weaver, with tremendous emphasis, as he was wont to do when feeling his opponent to be full of scepticism and doubt.

" When I say you are a fool, Weaver, I really don't mean to insult you : I merely wish to illustrate the word."

" When I am landing you one on the chin, I do so entirely without malice. There," he said.

Proudfoot blinked. " You are right. I congratulate you on admirably illustrating the incommensurable qualities of our respective weapons of offence. Still, allow me to doubt the amount of a condemned man's enjoyment. An ex-warder told me once how out of ninety-eight executions he had witnessed there was not one case when the victim did not either collapse or was dragged fighting and screaming to the gallows. And the women, they cry and kick their heels as they are carried there. But the Press prints the official version that the prisoner ' walked firmly to the scaffold ' and that it was all over in less than twenty-five seconds."

" Still I am in favour of hanging," Weaver said, thoughtfully.

" No man has any right to be in favour of something the full horror of which he is, through his own defective imagination, incapable of realising."

" Abolish capital punishment, and nobody's life will be safe."

" Stupidity," said Mr. Proudfoot, " is in itself a hollow term : it is people like yourself who lend it meaning. Nobody's life will be safe ! " he mimicked derisively.

" Undoubtedly ! "

" This is what they said of sheep-stealing at the time. ' Abolish the death penalty for stealing sheep, and not a sheep will be left in this fair England of ours ! ' And all these little boys and girls who, in Queen Victoria's golden reign, were hanged for stealing a spoon. ' Abolish hanging,' the people said, ' and there will not be left a single silver spoon in England.' Oh, my God ! I'm ashamed of humanity....Little boys and girls...in the condemned cell...dragged out in the morning and hanged...in Victoria's complacent time—when Englishmen were ' good.' "

" Serve 'em right, the brats ! Teach 'em a lesson ! We had a case recently——"

" Devil ! " he said. " Devil ! " Mr. Proudfoot clutched the stick in his shaking fist—he was not to blame that the other end of it shook at a far greater tangent—and thus shaking it at one end touched Weaver's neck with the other. Even as he did so he had a feeling that he had overstepped the mark, and he was about to crave his friend's pardon— when he saw that he had indeed overstepped it. Weaver leaned back and turned his face to his friend as who might say, " Hello, old chap, what's up ? " But the singular thing was that Weaver remained sitting there with just the same astonished look in his face. Only blood was now trickling from the corner of his mouth down his new light-grey suit.

Proudfoot remembered how distinctly his senses registered the details of subsequent events. As he walked home one little boy out of a group of little boys and girls asked him for a cigarette card. He said he hadn't any and passed along, but the little boy ran after him and shouted, " Give me a cigarette card ! "

" *Haven't got any !* " he bellowed in reply.

And the little boy, frightened, began to cry softly.

" You shouldn't ask like that," he was consoled by his little sisters. " You should ask properly."

And suddenly Proudfoot felt that he was not the man to bellow now.

The tram-car was nearly empty. He would have preferred to have it full. A fat old woman was holding forth to the conductor, who punctuated her flowing narrative with periodical " Ay—ay's " : " 'Ad a real good time. Forty of us went to Blackpool in a sharry. It cost us ten bob a 'ead. Ee ! but we did 'ave a fine h'outing. An' such a dinner ! We started wi' lamb and green peas and fresh potatoes ; after that we 'ad potato pie, an' 'alf a chicken for each one of us, and pop to drink. After dinner we went for a picnic and took us tea wi' us. Eh, *'twas* a treat ! We 'ad three fine tongues all cut up an' ready like and plenty o' bread and butter. But th' pity was as I was off me h'appetite an' couldn't manage me share. When we was coming w'home we called at a pub or two, as we was very dry. Ee ! but it *was* a fine outing ! "

Wasn't life wonderful !

And suddenly Proudfoot remembered.

As he went down a narrow lane, a little girl said to a smaller one who had fallen on a stone, " Now you've made a 'ole in yer leg." And he felt that, in other circumstances, he might have smiled. Passing the grocer's, where Betty was still reading *Only a Mill Girl*, he wondered whether he should go in as if nothing had occurred and buy his usual packet of cigarettes. Or better not be seen. One less witness in court. What had he better do ? Now he was back in Pedlar-with-Thresham, and passing the familiar brass plate with " Gilbert French, Solicitor," he wondered whether he should go in, remembering the pun he used to make that Gilbert was a French solicitor. He somehow wished he was. He wished he himself were away in France. But they would extradite him on a warrant. Oh, God ! was there really no escape ?

Then things moved very quickly. He went home. The sun was still shining. His father was sitting in the garden which gave upon the street. The two men lived silently beside each other. They had never had much to say to each other. The father, when the boy first showed signs of an independent mind and temper and of wanting to adopt an unconventional career, warned him solemnly : " You'll come to a bad end,

young feller-me-lad!" Now the old man was very
old: so old that his thoughts—let alone his body—
stirred with difficulty. He sat all day long in the
sun and at intervals would make remarks such as:
"Ay, she is a strong wench she is," or "Ay, he is
a big man he is that." Then he would sit very still,
staring ahead with his watery old eyes, munching with
his empty loose mouth. Suddenly he would fall asleep,
his mouth hanging wide open. One day when he would
thus fall asleep they would nail him up in a coffin and
drive him at great speed to the graveyard, and put
him into a wet black hole and cover him up altogether
with earth, and plant a great heavy stone on the top
of him—and then come home and take tea.

"Just as well," Proudfoot reflected. "Just as well
now."

The sun had gone; it was just beginning to drizzle.
His father turned in. He sat by him and stared into
the fire, waiting for the police to come and arrest him.
They did not come, and unable to bear the suspense
any longer he went out to give himself up at the police
station. It was beginning to get dark and chilly out-of-
doors; the polluted rain fell out of a soot-infested sky;
and close to the door his courage failed him and he
went away again. What could he do? Where could

he go ? It seemed all one. Mrs. Weaver knew that they had gone out together and even knew the place. Was it really possible that such a thing had befallen him ? If it had befallen another man, if he had read about it in the papers, it would seem natural enough ; but that it should have befallen him ! It seemed impossible. The uncanny thing was that the others would not know how impossible it seemed to him and would require an intelligent account of it from him. Tired of walking, frustration on all sides staring him in the face, he turned home and was arrested by the two policemen who were already waiting for him.

The court next morning had no hesitation in charging him with wilful murder, and, in charge of two men, he was taken to Liverpool, where a grand jury brought in a true bill against him, and he was taken away to await trial at the Assizes. Here the matter was put elaborately before a grand jury, and he listened, bedraggled and bewildered, to his heinous deed being recounted in the hearing of the public and ably handled by the learned advocates ; and he had a sense of clumsy unreality, as he had had when attending the performance of his plays or reading in a printed notice the reviewer's brief narration of the plot of his own novel. All this, attributed to him, did not seem his, was not of

68

his own making. But he was hopeful: there was time enough for despair later on. He watched the prosecution unbend itself. A sly old fox counsel for the Crown. He put it to them that the circumstances were most suspicious. Prisoner had decoyed his victim into a lonely wood away up on the moors. The wound witnessed that the blow had been inflicted with a blunt and heavy weapon. Prisoner confessed as much. What more proof was needed of his murderous intent? Mr. Proudfoot's faith was in his counsel, as once upon a time when he visited the races it had been in his jockey. He had a reputation for an unbroken record of acquittals to sustain. He would fight for them both to the last breath. And the judge seemed a gentleman. Mr. Proudfoot had the same feeling of confidence in that presiding wigged figure as in the umpire when, as a boy, he took part in a lawn tennis tournament. But what was strange and uncanny was the smooth procedure of it: the deference and kindness shown to him on all sides. He was afraid that with that suave politeness, that unfailing legal gloss, in those beautifully modulated Oxford accents, they might bring him theoretically to within an inch of death, and then get the common churl to carry out the messy business.

The judge was really nice—and so witty. Mr. Proudfoot smiled good-naturedly at his remarks. He would have laughed too, but that might seem uncanny, irresponsible ; might be considered as bravado on his part ; might even strike the judge as bordering on contempt of court. But the judge must know that Mr. Proudfoot was an author and critic of standing and might be flattered if he saw that his witticisms were appreciated by the critic even at a trying time. The judge was detached by virtue of his training. He pictured him as an elderly cultured bachelor who had an ancient library and tender nieces who adored him. Mr. Proudfoot and the judge would get on very well together. It was the jurymen he was afraid of. God only knew in what wise the particular machinery in their skulls manipulated thought. Counsel for the Crown was a little ratty, to say the least of it. He would ask incriminating questions : Who killed him ? The devil killed him. He did not kill him. As if he, Joseph Proudfoot, would ever do such a thing. He had merely shaken his stick at him : the devil had opera-ted the other end of it. But if he had now told them that it was the devil who had killed Weaver, the jury, being of the type who prided themselves on not being born yes-terday, would all the sooner come to a conclusion of his

70

guilt. But murder him, he didn't—because murder had indeed never crossed his mind. But counsel for the Crown thought otherwise. He could see no trace of provocation to manslaughter, in the absence of which he saw murder, the possibility of self-defence not even being mentioned by the other side. And he suggested Mr. Proudfoot had murdered his friend for money.

" I suggest," he said, " that you murdered him for his money and took it."

"I repudiate your suggestion," Mr. Proudfoot said, very pale.

Counsel for the defence was stipulating for manslaughter under provocation, the provocation being Weaver's inhuman attitude to those poor children who, in Victoria's crass time, had been suffered by a callous public to forfeit their young lives at the hands of the hangman, a dastardly crime which Weaver had offensively condoned ; and this general attitude to juvenile capital punishment raised a tremendous controversy between the two sides, involving the merits of capital punishment as a whole, the defence representing it as a barbarous relic of a bygone age still lingering among us, and to which indeed his client may fall a ready victim if the jury did not do their duty by him ;

71

till the judge, resenting such roundabout intimidation
of the jury, said that they were not here to debate
whether the death penalty was right or wrong in
principle, but that the question which the jury had to
keep before them was whether prisoner had murdered
Weaver or killed him under justifiable provocation,
in which latter case it might be said it was manslaughter.
Whereupon counsel for the defence respectfully submitted to his lordship that the degree of provocation
would seem to be intimately bound up with his client's
sensitive and all-too-human—perhaps over-sensitive,
but he would hesitate to call it over-human—attitude
to a practice which to-day all right-thinking people
("Hear, hear!" from the audience, the judge inter-
rupting to say that at the repetition of outside comments
he would clear the court)—yes, he repeated it advisedly,
all right-thinking people could but recall with a shudder
of horror and disgust; and the learned judge (the point
at issue having crystallised itself by now) allowed the
argument to stand, limiting it strictly to the merits
of the death penalty as applied to children for stealing
silver spoons at a particular period in social history.
Prosecuting counsel, in his turn, submitted that if
there was any provocation at all, even of a kind that
some people—though he himself was far from doing

so—might find, if not a ground, at least an extenuating circumstance for taking the life of another human being, they had only the prisoner's word for it. It was a matter of credulity. He repeated the assertion of the learned counsel for the defence in a faintly ironic tone, and added that he would ask the jury to please declare the prisoner innocent of murder—if they could honestly believe it. (He implied by a shade of sarcasm, if they were really simple enough to believe such a wild thing.) Mr. Proudfoot cast a quick glance at the jury. Two jurymen, looking singularly like Messrs. Asquith and Lloyd George, he thought, mingled their locks in contemptuous mirth. They seemed men with " no nonsense about them," men who would ask, " Do you see any green in my eye ? " men who were prone to be-lieve that " there is no smoke without fire," men who had sent saints to the stake ; men of whom Mr. Proudfoot all of a sudden had become immoderately afraid. If they could believe such a thing, the prose-cution argued, there was an end of it and he had nothing further to say. But if they did not, indeed *could* not believe it, and there was no provocation, he said (sudden-ly jumping one peg), then, he submitted, it was murder pure and simple.

The proceedings made a web of rather illiberal

quibbles, difficult for any but a trained mind to unravel, but through all the crude, inaccurate and intellectually dishonest cross-examinations there ran two threads : the black thread of the prosecution and the white thread of the defence, which the jury hoped the judge would disentangle for them in his summing-up. Unable to sustain the charge that prisoner had taken any of the victim's money (though producing witnesses to show that Proudfoot was in financial embarrassment), prosecuting counsel modified it to saying that he *would* have taken it, but in the horror of the crime itself forgot the object of the crime. The defence thereupon came forward with a challenge to the prosecution either to substantiate the charge or to withdraw it—a challenge which the prosecution met with a subversive question : Indeed what other rational cause could have prompted prisoner to commit the murder ? A question retorted to by the defence with the suggestion that the absence of all rational motive precisely pointed to the view that apparently it was not murder, but manslaughter under some sharp and instantaneous provocation, which tallied with his client's story. But prosecuting counsel knew his jurymen, and questioning whether the expression of a contradictory opinion on some event in history could be described as provocation, and questioning further whether prisoner could be believed to tell the truth, he wound up his case with a pseudo generous invitation to the jury to exercise their credulity if they possessed enough of it, in believing the case for the defence. Again Mr. Proudfoot glanced at the jury : hard-faced business men all, " with no nonsense about them," and one meagre " emancipated " woman who looked as though she would not lag behind the men. " My God, my God, why hast Thou forsaken me ? "

He stared in front of him. Now they seemed very near, and now they seemed very far, as if he were looking at them through the other end of a pair of binocular glasses. He started from his trance : Good God ! he was actually in court, being tried, in fact, for his life !

He found the final speech for the defence inadequate. These lawyers were all so suave and satisfied with one another : his man, while fighting for his life, seemed so mindful of the prosecution, so gentlemanly, so aware of his opponent's high character and diverse gifts that Mr. Proudfoot felt his barrister might easily betray him to his foe out of gracious deference and general drawing-room politeness. So on the declaration of a war, the signal for the indiscriminate butchery all round of human flesh, ambassadors who had demanded the return of their credentials will cordially shake hands with the immaculate kid-gloved Foreign Secretary, before departing to the country with which the realm is " in a state of war." " This," said Sir Frederick, laying down his brief, " concludes the case for the defence."

And now he felt there was only God between him and his doom.

Among men, who was his friend? Not the judge, you would think any more, if you followed the hostile tone of his summing-up : the arguments themselves were far too intricate for any layman not specially versed in legal ways to follow. And Proudfoot wondered which of all his friends he would want to help him in his present plight ; and he thought that of all men he wanted the good, fat, cheery, smiling Weaver. And a laugh broke from his mouth and tears came to his eyes as he remembered that all the present trouble hinged on Weaver.

There was a moment during the judge's summing-up when something in Proudfoot protested. What right had they to sit in judgment on him? " I have under-standing as well as you. I am not inferior to you. Yea, who knoweth not such things as these ? " That ridiculous wigged figure, immune from insult, sitting aloft impersonating the divine justice. He felt like telling it, " You old cuckoo, you wouldn't be sitting there if it weren't that you are only half a man."

The jury retired. How very long ! It seemed as though they would never come to an unanimous decision. He had hopes of disagreement, procrastination, a new trial. But at last they came back, headed by the foreman. He heard the clerk's fateful question. He heard the answering " Guilty." There was no recommendation for mercy. Before he could take it in he saw the " black cap " on the judge's wig. "...hanged by the neck until you are dead...." The judge and all of them seemed very far off in the electric light, as if at the far end of a long hall. He could not believe it, he did not believe it. Absurd ! They were wanting to despatch him, to liquidate his existence : whereas he was the world spirit itself, the world spirit that des- cends into each living creature whole and unsplit : as if each creature only mattered by itself and no other creature. To be told that you are to be killed is there- fore like being told that the end of the world has come : impossible to fathom. They must be under some error. They had forgotten that he was the world spirit incapable of being quenched by a judge of that kind. The judge's slender hand moving up, the clerk removed the piece of black cloth from his lordship's wig. It seemed that all was over. The judge was thanking the jury for the commendable manner in which they had carried out their duties and was absolving them from further service for the next fifteen years. He felt the warder's hand on his shoulder; they led him down to the cells; afterwards out into a taxi, the two warders inside with him. He looked out of the window as they were wafted down busy streets; past door porters at picture palaces who looked like major-generals; then through shabbier streets. He still looked out. An auctioneer was holding forth outside his shop, talking vociferously but apparently to himself.

Then the bath at the prison. The kindness of the warders. It was like a working men's hotel. He could smile—and there was plenty of time—two weeks yet or more. He now lived in the hope that the High Court of Criminal Appeal would revoke the sentence. But the day came, and the Lord Chief Justice gave it out as his opinion that he could find no fault with the proceedings at the trial, and, speaking *ex cathedra*, added some mordant comments of his

own upon the class of novelists now generally per-
verting the public. The friend who brought the news
to him consoled him with the lame remark that it was
better to be hanged once than to be imprisoned for a
period of twenty years. After all, hanging was more
merciful.

" If it is," exclaimed Mr. Proudfoot, feeling chilly
at his friend's taking his death so philosophically,
" if it is, and they are so solicitous as to what is better
for me, why don't they let me make my choice ?
I know what I would choose."

" What ? "

" Life imprisonment, of course. I am locked up,
but I can still think, my thoughts can still roam, my
mind is still free and unfettered."

" That is the cowardly choice, not the good choice."

" I am only human," said Proudfoot—and faltered.

There came a time, after the High Court had dismissed
his appeal, when he felt quite light and cheery in the
confident anticipation of the Home Secretary's inter-
vention. He thought of the Home Secretary as a man
with a soft grey moustache and kind eyes. But just
as he had feared the suave punctilio of the trial, he
began to fear the sensitive, kind hearted men, who,
wincing in their sensibilities, would turn aside and

leave it to the other men to deal with the raw places. He read of the Home Secretary going off for his customary week-end ; he learnt of his solicitor travelling to him with a batch of signatures, and coming back, ambiguous in the extreme, only saying that the Home Secretary's decision would be duly published after his return to London from his week-end holiday. Then he saw it in the morning papers. The Home Secretary could see no ground for advising his Majesty to intervene with the normal course of the sentence, and the papers further stated that the sheriff had arranged for the excution to take place on the 22nd of this month, and that on the morning of the 21st, Hanbury, the executioner, would travel to Liverpool to put up the gallows.

And then he asked—it was a desperate after-thought —that they should let him finish his new novel. It was all but ready ; he only asked two weeks' respite. Secretly he hoped that it might be found so good that all the writers and critics in the world and the Great British (Reading) Public would see to it that he was granted life. It was an application truly without precedent. But there was nothing lost by trying. There was still time, and his solicitor got busy. The petition was drawn up and had appended to it a long list of signatures from all the leading lights in letters, music, art and science, some from the dramatic stage, and not a few illustrious foreigners from France and Italy, even one from Poland and Czecho-Slovakia. A German writer's name was intentionally omitted from the list, as it was feared that a certain daily paper would be sure to cry out that opinion in this country was being dictated from Berlin, and that the convalescent mind of our post-war public might echo the cry, and the Government would find it difficult to grant the application.

However, the respite was granted. It was his first success after a long series of reverses. He had another two weeks clear to finish his book in. Some newspapers of the howling kind, duly howled against it. "What Can Murderers Teach Us?" was the headline of a certain Sunday paper. "Why, to murder," he could almost hear the responding voice of certain readers. "Writers are worse than some other folk," he could just hear them saying it in Pedlar-with-Thresham. "Ay, they are a bad lot." And Mrs. Weaver answering, "That's right."

He remembered how she had sat in court, saying in reply to a question put to her by counsel, "That's right," and never once looked up at him.

The book was got out with all haste. Three days before the execution it was published, and his publisher sent him the first batch of reviews. The stimulus given to it by his impending execution was tremendous. His publisher recognised it as an invaluable advertisement and rose to the occasion. For the first time in his life Mr. Proudfoot was a rich man, and he made generous provision for his father, for the few years that he could yet be expected to survive. But the integrity of the British reviewer is proverbial. The mere fact of Proudfoot's impending death could not influence their critical opinion of his work one way or another. One critic wrote: " This book, while quite pleasant and readable, is in no way remarkable," and another critic, ignorant, it would seem, of the fate involved, pleaded: " Go back, get you back to your former style, and we shall listen to you till the crack of doom." He *had* gone back; he had deliberately gone back on the advice of that same critic, and in any case there was no looking forward now. But still another critic wrote : " One would wish the author had begun to break new ground, express life from a new angle...." The Great British Public was silent as the grave.

The last hope had gone, and the last full day of

his remaining life was beginning to unfold itself. The warders, like old friends, played cards with him all day to take his mind off from the event. In the little intervals he wondered whether Hanbury who was to hang him on the morrow was not perchance the man who bit off the heads of live rats whom he and Weaver should have visited that fatal Sunday. Weaver had not disclosed his name. But there were few hangmen, he knew, and this might very well be the man in question. " Where does Hanbury, the hangman, come from ? " he inquired from the warder.

" Up Manchester way."

It *was* the man !

What emotions, what a multitude of moods he experienced in those few brief hours. Till twelve he was sprightly and not very nervous. The hangman, peeping at him through the observation hole, to decide what " drop " to give him, saw him pacing up and down in the cell, puffing calmly at a cigarette. But as, at midnight, the prison clock boomed out the hours, he got agitated, threw away the cigarette and began counting the remaining hours on his fingers. He tried to think of the noble souls who went before him :— of Anton Chehov, who, after gravely saying to the doctor who had been called to him during the night,

"I am dying," drinking the glass of champagne prescribed to him to the bottom and remarking, with a smile, to his wife, "It's a long while since I have had champagne," turning over on one side, and presently being quiet for ever;—of Goethe asking that the window might be opened to admit of more air and more light, and the faithful Eckermann coming to look at him, lying dead. "And I turned aside," he records, "to give a free run to my tears." And with a shudder he recalled that *his* body would fall into lime to be instantly consumed like a foul thing. He must go not knowing why he lived, and nobody in those bleak immensities would know or care : no father, no mother, no love in the world would intervene on his behalf; not even memory would be left him to recall his single spell of life, as if he never had been, as if indeed he was never meant to matter. There was but to "curse God and die."

And suddenly his soul stirred within him, as if it had wings. "It's the end here," he thought. "But it's not the end there." Weaver believed in the world-soul—which meant that in a while he and Weaver would be one. It was night, but he could not sleep. Perhaps now, all over the world, there were people who could not sleep on his account and lay thinking

84

of him. As by imponderable wireless waves he, alone in the dark cell with the gallows adjoining, felt himself linked to all compassionate souls ; and to them he sent greetings—his desperate greetings.... At last he slept.

His sleep was troubled. He dreamt he had shrunk back from the pale gate of death, a bleak coldness in his chest and limbs, and was going past a park where there were children playing and people lounging wearily after their strenuous day's work. And he thought that the trivialities of living were manna compared with death. But by the faces of the people who came out of the park he knew that they, not realising it, could not enjoy the gift of life. He walked on, and suddenly found himself in a beautiful, totally unfamiliar part of the town, the existence of which he had not even suspected. And he told himself how he would come home and tell his father of it. He woke—and there was nothing to tell but that he had dreamt it. And at once an incredible coldness invaded his heart.

Besides, it was cold in the cell. Our courage is at its lowest ebb in the early morning : it is wicked to hang people at dawn, he reflected. The warder came in. " Get up. Here is your suit." His old suit that knew him in different circumstances. No collar to-day. " I'll go and fetch you yer breakfast now."

Perhaps at the last minute the Home Secretary might...? He remembered seeing a film where also at the last moment, also the Home Secretary... How cold. They wouldn't tell his father. Or would they ? The warder brought in a tray with some cocoa and porridge and an apple. He could not eat. He nibbled at the apple, and the savoury juice reminded him of some utopian land of fruit and flowers, like Italy, which he had never known. And he thought that when they had done their worst, and he was left in peace, perhaps in dreamland he would fly to such a land.

He looked strangely at the warder. " Is it very bad ? Does it...hurt ? " he asked uneasily.

" No. A second and it's all over. Like having yer tooth out—no more. All over in a wink."

The chaplain, a young man, was more confused than he—and more miserable. " Perhaps some spiritual consolation ? " he stammered.

" I don't understand," said Mr. Proudfoot. " The indivisible universe speaks and lives only through each separate creature, as if no other creature existed at all. But it is the same indivisible universe which so expresses itself. And they—absurd—they want to do away with me—that means with the universe."

" Perhaps a last communion..."

" Why ? "

" Or a confession ? After all, you've killed a human being."

He thought of Weaver, and would have felt sorry for him if he did not feel so overwhelmingly sorry for himself. If they'd let him off now he'd put back what he had taken, put back into the spiritual cosmos what he'd taken from it. If they would leave it to him, he'd see that humanity did not lose.

He was brave, resigned. But a quarter of an hour before time, suddenly he felt he wanted to live, love, breathe in through these nostrils the fresh air of, not this, but other, future mornings, when *he* would be no more.... He remembered a windy day when the big chestnuts swayed and lashed their branches like drunken things, and nuts and sticks fell off like missiles aimed at passers-by. A little boy had turned round to his mother, hiding his eyes from the dust and the wind in the folds of her skirt. This had moved him then somehow. And now an intolerable thought obsessed him that, when, in a few minutes from now, he would be buried in a pool of lime, he would feel the wind no more. And he thought that if this life he was leaving was the only life in a bleak universe, then he could not face the anguish of leaving it. But if there was another life, he wanted to hide his face in the lap of his Maker, hide from the missiles that fell all about him and hurt him, weep on His breast, and be quiet for ever....

But perhaps—two minutes yet—perhaps the Home Secretary...? And before he could realise it the hangman stood in the cell. Was this it? Was it this? Was *this*, then, what he had come to? Could mother but have known! But the warder, who up to this had been like a friend and confidant, suddenly began to shout at the executioner, "Come on, you there, get a move on and get about it quick!" (as though anxious to get the nasty job over). And Mr. Proudfoot felt almost as though his friend the warder had betrayed him to that other man. That other man had a soft, drooping, yellow moustache and glassy eyes, and seemed slow and good-natured. You wouldn't think by the look of him that he bit off the heads of live rats. Somehow Mr. Proudfoot wanted to claim acquaintance: to tell him about Weaver: that Weaver and himself were about to call on him that fatal Sunday : if they had called he would not now be here. But the man with his assistant and the warder were resolutely coming up to him as if they were intent on making a swift end of him, the governor, the chaplain and the doctor looking on. Yes, yes, he would die—if they would leave him alone, or do it—handsomely. He killed Weaver—however inadvertently, he killed him, and he would forfeit his life, on his word of honour he would. But not so—— The hangman and his assistant were trying to pinion him ; and suddenly he put up a fight for his life. What right had they ? All nonsense apart, what right ? A glimpse of the jurymen all back in their homes, and at breakfast, flashed through his brain ? What right ? Where he got the strength from he did not know, but the prison bell was already tolling for the soul departing, and its last stroke had boomed its melancholy message across the yard into the streets, but Mr. Proudfoot was still alive and struggling desperately with the executioner and three warders, who only knew that they had to despatch him : he should have been liquidated ten minutes ago : there was no document to account for his unwarranted existence after 8 a.m. They were shocked : it was improper in the extreme. " Don't ! Oh ! " He wanted to tell

them—if they would only stop to listen—he wanted
to tell them that—yes—he was a soul, a universe
with things in it which had nothing to do with that
devil in him they were intent on destroying. It was
unjust. A whole universe. " Stop ! Think : what are
you doing ?...*No !* " he cried, struggling in their
grip and realising that nothing save his poor physical
exertion now stood between him and their grim
determination to do away with him. " No ! You
mustn't ! " he pleaded, his soul filled with a sickening
animal fear. But they dragged him on without respite,
the chaplain leading the way, reading words from the
Bible. And if—he thought—there was a God in
heaven, why did He stand aside ? What God was He
to stand aside ? " No ! No !...*Oh !*..." But they
were dragging him on none the less, dragging him on
to his doom. Swiftly he looked at each of them, for a
spark of compassion. But they were all men who
valued their duty before everything else. He was in
the open. And suddenly a wave of awe came over him,
standing as he did on the brink of eternity or extinction :
so that the hangman at his neck seemed like a friend
who was assisting at a parting, and those others, too,
seemed as if they'd come to see him off at the railway
station as he was about to step into the train on his

awful journey ; and he clung to them with a fraternal, desperate farewell. But they only looked as though they had no time for that, but wanted to get the nasty business, long overdue, over at last. It seemed minutes before he toed the chalk line on the drop—when suddenly he fell, it seemed minutes, he expected it with drawn breath, the pulling up—when *snap !* it came !

And all was darkness.

The great harbour was awakening in the cold fog. From the terminus a tram-car set off half empty. The conductor strode inside and began collecting the fare. Then newspapers appeared on the street corners, and posters announced in red and black letters :

" Special Edition.
Proudfoot Executed."

They were eagerly snapped up by busy hurrying people, who stopped and read :

" Proudfoot had a quiet night and is believed to have been greatly relieved at the end by confessing his crime to the chaplain. The condemned man breakfasted lightly and walked with a firm step to the scaffold. From the moment of prisoner leaving his cell to the execution of the sentence there barely elapsed twenty-five seconds."

&

IN THE WOOD

LIEUTENANT BARAHMEIEV, late of the Hussars, was
making amorous advances to his landlord's wife,
a Jewish lady of about thirty. " Your lips are saying
No! No! No! whereas your eyes are saying Yes!
Yes! Yes!"

Vera Solomonovna looked at him with her golden
eyes and shook her handsome head and said to him:

" Boris Nikolàech, you're thirty-eight, and you have
no more sense than a boy of twelve."

Lieutenant Barahmeiev looked more self-confident
than ever. It was a fixed idea with him that no woman
could refuse his amorous advances, and that no landlord
really meant him seriously to pay his rent. To whatever women said in proof of their refusal, to whatever
landlords said in confirmation of their claims, Lieutenant
Barahmeiev had a simple answer. He called it " bluff."
Some English words like " bluff " and "gentleman "
have passed into the Russian tongue in the original.
He wasn't born yesterday, he said.

And fully confident of the result, the Russian officer

continued, " Why this pretence, this hypocritical reluctance ? Why not be frank about it ? To-night," he whispered. " In my room ..."

" Go to the devil ! " she said, but her eyes seemed to say, " Go on talking."

" You say ' Go to the devil ! ' But what do you mean ? I know what you mean. Wasn't born yesterday. Why not be honest about it ? "

Odessa had been changing hands from Bolshevik to anti-Bolshevik in turn ; but the habit of love-making persists through such irrelevancies as wars and revolutions. Life in the flat of Finkelstein, where Lieutenant Barahmeiev occupied a bedroom, went on essentially as it had gone on before the war. I liked my hosts. She, a woman of considerable beauty, greedy for admiration. He, a successful broker, tall, handsome, prepossessing, inordinately proud of being a Jew and always selling foreign currencies to his guests at table. I liked the free and easy manner in the household, the total absence of suspicion on the part of Finkelstein as regards his handsome wife. No doubt he also had no small opinion of himself, and thought that as compared with the Lieutenant he was the better specimen of male all round. And I think that perhaps he was.

At lunch he was saying to Lieutenant Barahmeiev,
" Yes, Boris Nikolàech, you Christians like to run us
down. You say that we are swindlers, and ' Never
trust a Jew.' But the fact is that we Jews can trust
each other, but I am dashed if we are often given an
opportunity to trust a Christian. Take yourself. You
call yourself a ' paying guest.' But what right have
you to the adjective ? If it comes to that, what right
have you to the noun ? Have I asked you to come
and stay with us, and overlooking that point, is it a
usual thing for guests to stay indefinitely ? But your
conscience doesn't seem to trouble you a bit. You eat
and sleep, and there ! you even seem to have designs on
my wife. Ah, you're a funny fellow, Boris Nikolàech,
but, at any rate, it's some good to us that you are an
officer ; it will keep them from commandeering our
flat while you are here. But what was I saying ?
Ah, yes, does anyone want to buy Romanov roubles ?
Or I can sell you francs."

But the Lieutenant went on talking to the hostess.
" What I can't get over is this utter want of frankness
in you, Vera Solomonovna. Your soul, your eyes
cry out, ' Take me ! I am yours ! ' whereas your
lying lips pretend to say, ' Go to the devil.' Bluff !
All bluff, all bluff ! "

94

She turned to her husband and looking at her guest with compassion, said:

"What *can* I do with him, Lyova? He doesn't understand. He *can't*. He really thinks he's irresistible to women. I've never seen anything so brazen in my life. To be quite frank, Boris Nikolàech, you're not the least bit attractive. I wonder who put that idea into your head?"

"Vera Solomonova," he implored her, "be frank for once. You know you are in love with me; why all this hypocritical nonsense about my being 'not the least bit attractive'? Why all this bluff? I wasn't born yesterday!"

"In matters of love you are a school boy."

"Yes, when I was a school boy I had the innocence to take a woman's No for No. But now, I need hardly say, I believe it no longer."

"You wise old man then," she said ironically, rising.

We followed her into the drawing-room. The window panes were blurred with rain. The sea, the sky, was one grey mass, doleful and monotonous. Below, in the street, one could see the shining hoods of passing cabs; the muffled sound of hoofs reached our windows. In the indoor twilight of the flat one felt at rest, one's limbs were seized with languor. Finkelstein and his stock-exchange associates retired to his study to play cards.

"The rain reminds me, Vera Solomonovna," said the Lieutenant, "of an incident in my youth. The woman—oh, she had the self-same psychology, if I may say so, as yourself, and in the end, and in the end...complete capitulation."

"I am tired of you," said she, looking languorous rather than tired.

"Vera Solomonovna," he said, bending over her; then in a whisper: "Don't forget to-night... my room."

She shook her head.

"How blatantly deceitful woman really are," he said. "You shake your head. Why? Why, when I know——"

She flushed. "This is really getting idiotic!"

"Ha! ha! ha! That is exactly what Zina used to say, 'idiotic.' I was going to tell you about Zina when you interrupted me. This was a long time ago —let me see—yes, twenty-one years ago, to be exact. I was seventeen then. I was a cadet at the X—— Military School and I was spending the summer vacation with my aunt at S——, a seaside resort some twenty miles from Petersburg. It was an evening in early June, and we were sitting on the open balcony of the pavilion at the local tennis club. We were discussing something—literature, I think, and then, quite relevantly, we switched off on to love. There was this Zina I am telling you about, a beautifully developed girl of twenty-five, who was quite vehement in her denunciation of everything relating to the attraction between the sexes, and as she spoke it was urged upon her that for a person with her views the convent was the only proper place. It was a lovely night, but we sat there and exchanged inanities. Gradually some of us dispersed.

I was standing by a street stall, buying cigarettes, when I noticed Zina coming up. She bought herself some chocolate. We sauntered away from the stall together.

" Where are you going ? " I asked her.

" Nowhere in particular."

We went along the big road leading to the sea.

Our shoulders touched occasionally as we stumbled over the uneven ground.

" They're so absurd with their revolting sentimentality," I said.

" Why talk about them ? Look at the clouds,"

97

she said. " How they chase each other. We couldn't keep pace with them if we ran. And the moon ! Gone —and out again ! "

We made our way together along a narrow lane. The wooden *datchas* had been left behind.

" Is this the ' Alley of Kisses ' ? "

" No, this is ' The Alley of Sighs.' "

We went on.

" The moon again ! "

" Yes."

" This is ' The Alley of Kisses,' " she said, as we turned to our left. Beyond I could hear the sound of the sea.

" Let us sit down here."

It was an old bench considerably disfigured by a penknife ; it bore initials, monograms and names of lovers who had sat there in former times.

" So this is ' The Alley of Kisses,' " I repeated. One seizes with gratitude on such openings.

" Yes," she looked at me strangely. " And the fools at the tennis club talking rubbish ! "

" Yes.

" The sea and the air ! and—as I was saying—this ' Alley of Kisses.' Can you feel it ? "

I moved closer to her. " May I kiss you ? " I said.

98

" Why do you ask ? " she whispered.

" What ? " said I. (I am slightly deaf, as you know.)

She waited, and I, timid, added, " After all, we are
' allies ' in a sort of way..."

She repeated softly : " Why do you ask ? "

She had soft, warm lips; I held my breath back;
it was long before I released it ; and I wasn't thinking
of the night. My hand——"

Vera Solomonovna became fidgety with excitement.
" Lyova ! Lyova ! " she cried out ; and when Finkelstein appeared, she said, " Come here, all of you.
Boris Nikolàech is telling of a romantic episode from
his life. It's most attractive, I assure you, most
piquant."

Finkelstein and his stock-exchange associates, aban-
doning their game of cards, sauntered into the drawing-
room, and, still smoking, sank into chairs and stretched
out their legs, ready to listen.

" Well, go on," said Vera Solomonovna.

" My hand, I think I said, was round her waist——"

" Whose waist ? " said Finkelstein.

" Zina's," explained his wife.

" Who's Zina, anyhow ? "

" Oh, well, it doesn't matter. Go on, Boris Nikolàech."

" My hand was round her waist.   She pressed it to her bosom.   I looked round.   There was not a soul around, not a sound abroad but for the waves that broke on the sea-shore.   Dark clouds ran swiftly across the sky.

" Let us go there," she said, pointing to the wood. We made our way across the shrubbery.   I held her in my arms ; she began to breathe in a queer, panting way.

" What is it ? " I asked ignorantly.

" It's...good," she whispered.

The moon showed between the tall trees ; at a few yards' distance the sea roared before us.   Then a big, heavy drop of rain fell on my face—it was warm ; and then another.

I sat on the moss, dazed, completely overtaken by the wonder of it all.   Suddenly, I heard the rustle of her movements ; she had disappeared behind a bush.

" What are you doing ? "

There was no answer.   I was rather shy about it all, for I was only seventeen.   " Don't ! "

She stood behind a shrub and I could hear the rustle of the twigs, the rustle of silk linen, the hollow sound of press-studs.   " Don't," I said.

" Yes," she whispered.

" But why ? Why ? " I said confusedly. " I don't want to."

Unveiled, she stood behind me. The big pale moon looked down upon her, but she didn't mind it. The dark blue wood leered from behind at her; and the roaring sea rushed to her—and receded, rushed and receded, moaning and crouching. Drop after drop, at long interval, the soft rain fell from the dark gathering clouds. " I want, I want you to remember me," she said softly, " *always*, and now you can't forget...that the first woman you have ever seen like that...was *me*." Then she crouched to the ground. She began to sob and laugh at the same time. " What am I doing ? Oh, I'm mad, mad...I couldn't help it. I've been reading all day long...such a wicked book. It was unbearable. These silly people on the veranda talked such nonsense, but it wouldn't have really mattered what they'd said ; I would have disagreed with them all the same. I couldn't bear it any longer. And then I felt I wanted —I wanted to do as she, the woman in the book, had done to him. Besides," she added, " you really are rather attractive, aren't you ? Oh, do you think it's going to rain properly ? It didn't in the book."

The Lieutenant ceased.

" Well ? " we said. " Go on."

" That's all," said the Lieutenant.

" But what happened afterwards ? " asked Vera Solomonovna.

" Nothing happened."

" But *how* ? " she said in a tone as though she had been wronged.

" Well, that's all there is to tell."

" But—it's no proper story even."

" I can't help that," he answered almost angrily. " This is what happened, and this is where it ended. I can't falsify the facts to suit your taste. We don't, my dear Vera Solomonovna, live our lives to provide plots for stories."

" Well, I *am* disappointed in you, Boris Nikolàech. Really ! To begin so well, so fascinatingly, and then, suddenly, to break off...so shamelessly ! Well, really, you're just like a boy of twelve. You have no sense of proportion, Boris Nikolàech, None whatever ! The whole thing as it stands is silly..."

" You are a hopeless washout ! " Finkelstein was teasing him. " Miss your opportunity like that ! My goodness ! And call yourself a Don Juan at that ! "

" If that's the end of it," said Vera Solomonovna, " there was no need to tell the story. You had no business to begin, Boris Nikolàech. It's simply disappointing."

"Well," said Lieutenant Barahmeiev, who seemed hurt, "if it comes to disappointment, I think I have been disappointed more than anyone."

"The more fool you," said Finkelstein.

"Nothing to do with me. Didn't I tell you it was raining?"

"Raining?"

"Pouring! It came on suddenly, burst upon us through the sky. A flood. The revenge of heaven on us."

"But what's the point of your story, anyhow?" asked Finkelstein.

"The point?"

"Yes, the moral? Why have you been telling it?"

"Oh, well, I told it to Vera Solomonovna by way of illustrating the psychology of women, because, like Zina, she affects derision of human passion, calls my amorous advances 'idiotic'; but just you wait and before the day is up—— There you are!"

Vera Solomonovna rose and left the room.

"There," said Finkelstein, "you've disgusted Vera."

" Disgusted her ! Ha ! ha ! Don't you believe it. Bluff ! my dear fellow. All bluff. You don't know women."

" You're a funny fellow, Boris Nikolàech. One can't say you're altogether stupid, but there are things you simply cannot understand. Impossible to penetrate yon marble brow of yours ; it's just like throwing a rubber ball at a stone wall : jumps back at you every time. And you don't know women. To take my wife, for instance. She's had enough of you already ; she's gone back to her bedroom in disgust."

" To *her* bedroom ? " questioned the Lieutenant in a derisive tone of voice.

" You don't expect her to go to yours, do you ! "

" Why...Oh, well, really, my dear fellow, I can see that you don't know women—although you've got a wife. Believe me, I know a thing or two about them. Wasn't born yesterday. Disgusted ! Ha, ha, ha ! You wait till I finish my cigarette and retire to my bedroom. You may be sure she's——"

" Boris Nikolàech," said Finkelstein, looking at him tranquilly through the smoke from his cigar, " you are an optimist."

And, looking dignified and prepossessing, he sauntered

over to his study where his stock-exchange associates were already waiting for him to resume their game of cards.

"Just a moment..." muttered the Lieutenant, "...finish my cigarette...."

&

THE VANITY-BAG

& I

IT was not that *he* thought her beautiful; but other people thought so, which made him think of her as such. And when these others came in swarms to wrest the prize from him which he had looked on as his own, he fell in love with her. During his first week in Salzburg, he received a card from Frau von Kranich:
"*As you whish to be introdused to interesting people, I would like to bring you on Monday next on the 15 February inst. to Professor Hollmann-Blum where there will be a pretty large party. Please komme to me at a quarter to five o'clock P.M. We will go together or better still, in the tramcar. With my kind regards yours truly,—Emmy von Kranich.*"

Calling, he beheld in the drawing-room with Frau von Kranich a young girl with clean-cut regularly chiselled features—he remembered later—of a quite extraordinary beauty. After introducing them: "Mr. Mackintosh Beck, of America. Miss Schulz," Frau von Kranich suddenly excused herself and went

106

out. There was a pause. " What the devil can I say ? "
he thought.

" Do you dance a great deal ? " He felt this was a
happy shot.

" No," said the girl.

" I notice that you Austrians dance very differently
from us, and I have, so as not to feel provincial "
(he smiled : the girl did not), " gone in for dancing
lessons at Herr Pfleger's—despite my middle age ! "
(Again she did not smile.) " I am told, on good
authority, that he is better than Herr Loewe."

" No," said the girl. " Loewe is better than Pfleger."

" But I think Herr Pfleger dances better than Herr
Loewe," he proffered tentatively.

The girl smiled a faint smile, as if of compassion for
Mr. Beck's poor understanding. " No," she said.
" Loewe dances better than Pfleger."

There was an end of it. Mr. Beck was silent. Frau
von Kranich came back with an enigmatic look on her
face which implied : " Well, have you two young people
hit it off ? " And Mr. Beck felt sensitive for Fräulein
Schulz, for, beside her, he was no longer young. But
Frau von Kranich was so old that from the vantage-
ground of her years the ages of both Mr. Beck and
Fräulein Schulz seemed quantities so small as to appear

to have no visible differentiation. She overtly began the matchmaking. " You must take long walks together in the spring as soon as the snow begins to thaw. She must show you round the lakes and up the hills." Now that Frau von Kranich, who had no illusions about the hearts of young girls, was back, Fräulein Schulz ceased to be assertive and became the shy and diffident young maiden Frau von Kranich must have thought her. When called upon to speak, she blushed and lowered her lashes. They put on their coats. Frau von Kranich, very small and old, and carrying a little pot of flowers in pink tissue-paper, crawled into the tramcar, Mr. Beck after her, and Fräulein Schulz, murmuring " Kiss the hand," went her way.

" She's a beautiful girl—he, he," said Frau von Kranich. The trolley rattled on. " She is a Cinderella who is waiting for the golden coach to halt at her door and for the Prince Charming to alight and offer her the shoe." And she pierced him searchingly with her sharp watery old eyes, as if considering whether he might conceivably pass off as the desired Prince Charming, and laughed—" He, he, he ! "

When they had crawled out of the tram and crawled upstairs into the flat, they made their way into a hall overcrowded by people's overcoats, and added to the huge stack, with the aid of a bewildered parlour-maid, their own particular contribution. Frau von Kranich crawled towards the festive birthday table heaped with flowers and deposited thereon the pot in the pink tissue-paper.

"Ah! ah! Herr Direktor Schulz!" A tall massive man of sixty-five, with long silver locks, stood in the doorway and now sat down by Frau von Kranich and talked to her, his big hands moving all the while in little gestures. Mr. Beck, amid the hum of conversation, was grateful for such fragments as his ear could catch. "This invidious meanness...this—this... mean invidiousness...this—how shall I say?" Herr Schulz was saying, when Frau von Kranich introduced them. "Sit down," she said. "He-he-he; you are so tall!"

Mr. Mackintosh Beck *was* tall. He was not handsome, but he thought he was; and when at home in Philadelphia the shop-girls stared at him behind the counter he thought they were admiring his features. From time to time, when, trying on a new suit at his tailor's, for example, he beheld his face in the three mirrors simultaneously from all four sides, he would experience a mild shock of revelation.

But as a rule he would forget about his looks and go on figuring himself as he should have been instead of as he really was. "You can speak French with Mr. Mackintosh," Frau von Kranich told Herr Schulz.

"As a matter of fact," Mr. Beck rejoined, smiling shyly through his horn-rimmed spectacles, "I am here to learn the German language, and I should esteem it a privilege to have the opportunity of exercising my poor knowledge if you have the patience to talk it slowly to me."

But Frau von Kranich looked as though she had something more important up her sleeve and was not to be deflected from her course. "French," she said, "is the most wonderful language that I know for telling one *des plaisanteries*. I remember how, while my father was Bavarian Minister at Rome, the French Ambassador and I talked airy nothings for an hour and a half—he, he, he!" And she looked round at Mr. Beck to see if he had noticed it. But Mr. Beck was looking at Herr Schulz and thinking of his daughter. He thought of the last girl he should have married and reflected, with a twinge of melancholy, that it was always girls who were to blame for the deflections in his career. He had wanted to remain at Haverford and prepare for a professorship, then a girl came in sight and he had to think of making money quickly. He left the University and took to banking. Then she left him, he ceased banking and went back to the University. And—strange, he thought—every time he was engaged it always happened that the cause of their estrangement was a male relative, a brother, father or an uncle whom, as a human being, he liked better than the girl. He was just thinking now, as he looked at Herr Direktor Schulz, how really strange it was that he should always like the fathers or the brothers best, when the host came up to him : " You come from Philadelphia ? Which University ? And what is your particular faculty ? "

" Well—my home town is Haverford, but I live in Philadelphia. My University——"

But Professor Hollmann-Blum, with a little nod and smile, was already off and round the corner, his coat tails flying in the air, and talking to another guest.

After coffee, the Professor gave a little lecture and passed on pictures of Tut-an-Khaman ; after which each of the more learned guests was expected to contribute his intellectual quota.

" I am a lonely soul here," said Herr Schulz.

" I felt that," Mr. Beck rejoined, and glanced significantly at Herr Schulz, who looked as if he did not quite take it in ; though when later he discoursed again, he turned with deference to the foreigner, and praised America. He spoke haltingly, with little gestures, little pauses, as if fumbling for the right word, and a number of people had gathered round him, but Herr Schulz turned more and more towards Mr. Beck. " When we are alone I should like to develop " (he threw out illuminative little gestures) " before you the whole idea, so to speak."

" And who is the greatest living writer of the German-speaking world to-day ? " presently asked Mr. Beck.

Herr Schulz smiled, a little mischievously. " With my exception " (and Frau Kranich also smiled) " it's Gerhart Hauptmann."

" The Herr Direktor is a poet," she explained.

" Oh ? "

" I will present you with a copy of my book when next we have the opportunity of meeting."

The Professor suddenly bobbed up from round the corner, and turning deferentially towards his host, the Herr Direktor, said : " The Herr Geheimrat will be able to reply to your question, Herr Doktor Mackintosh, with an authority greatly in excess of that which I command."

" What's that ? What's that ? " asked the Professor, joining them as if for a long stay.

" We were talking of——"

But the Professor, with a nod and a smile, had already dashed off to the table in the other corner of the room and was fussing with a fork over the apricot cake.

Mr. Beck escorted the old lady home. " I like Herr Schulz," he said.

" He's very nice to you because you are a new man, a foreigner at that, and listen to him—and that flatters him. While we have all heard it endless times before and are sick and tired of it ; and he knows it. But I will bring his daughter, Irmgard Schulz, for you to the Baroness Hauch's dance on Thursday afternoon. Baroness Hauch has the finest china set in Salzburg."

" Must I dress ?"

" Yes."

" Dinner jacket ? "

" No—cut-away."

& II

THE trouble was that Mr. Beck possessed no " cut-away." Accordingly, he had one made, and standing facing the three glasses at the front, with his back against three more, he suddenly perceived that he was very ugly. The tailor looked at him with glee. " American ? Ah ! ah ! Dollar ! A lot of dollar—he, he, he ! " and recommended the most expensive stuff available, while Mr. Beck reflected with discomfort that not the least of his reasons in coming over to Austria was the resolve drastically to reduce expenditure. " Have the honour—kiss the hand—my compliment —great God—commend myself," the tailor bowed him out. In the afternoon Mr. Beck dropped cards on Baroness Hauch, on the door of whose apartment he read : " Baron Karl Franz Egon Gaestner zu Hauch Wolf-Kadelburg von Hofmannsthal," and on Thursday, as arranged, he called on Frau von Kranich. Irmgard came. In her brown hat which covered her exquisitely moulded forehead she did not look quite so lovely, and he noticed that she had the small burning eyes of her father. At the Hauchs' Irmgard appeared a little shy. She wore a blue dress with white lapels and American brown shoes, and all the young men fell in love with her at first sight and danced with her uninterruptedly. Mr. Beck found himself seated far away from the table, with a cup of tea in his hand. There was no sugar in the tea, but the cup was too full and too hot ; he knew he could never get up without spilling it—and he suffered in silence. Moreover, he remembered being told that the Baronin Hauch possessed the finest china set in Salzburg and he was tormented by the thought that at any moment he might drop the cup and smash the precious cup to smithereens! And what then——? The hostess spoke agitatedly, with her mouth full of crumbs, and every now and then a crumb would be shot out of her mouth to fly like a bullet into the middle of the cakes and pies. "What a beautiful girl," she remarked, watching Irmgard dance with her son Franz Egnon Rudolf Ferdinand.

"She's just like a Cinderella," answered Frau von Kranich, "waiting for Prince Charming to claim her."

"But I hear," breathed a nondescript lady, "that her father is not liked because of his intolerable conceit. I am told that when someone asked him recently about German authors, Herr Direktor Schulz had the indiscretion to reply that he was by far the greatest writer living! And he looks as though he thought it —walking round in that old-fashioned trilby hat and the astrakhan coat, looking like an English lord."

Frau von Kranich wrinkled her nose. "He is a little bit of a *parvenu*," she said.

"I haven't noticed that," rejoined the Baroness, while a crumb shot from her mouth right into the sugar-basin.

"Still—a little."

They were beginning to play bridge—the princes seated in one room; the counts in another; the barons in a third, Mr. Beck among the barons, who spoke to him of the high purchasing power of the U.S. dollar and urged him to subscribe to various aristocratic charities. Frau von Kranich had long since gone away. When the gathering at last dispersed, he went with Irmgard to the tram, but she suggested walking home together to the castle. "I like walking after a dance."

Mr. Beck considered. "I like walking—with you." He thought this very daring. And he reflected, with inward satisfaction, that he was actually making love in German—for the first time in his uneventful life. It wasn't..."half bad!"

She paused. "I like—walking," she said.

This was cautious. And Mr. Beck put out feelers. "I don't want to impose myself on you, and please tell me when you've had enough of me."

"I'll tell you."

"I mentioned it because it seems to me that Frau

von Kranich is rather inflicting my heavy company upon your slender shoulders. Needless to say, for my own part I like it. At the same time, I feel I may be boring you with my imperfect German, and I'd do anything in the world rather than be a nuisance to you."

" She means well," said Irmgard ; and they walked along in silence through the frosty streets.

" Have you always lived in Salzburg, then ? "

" Always—since my birth."

" Do you like it ? "

" I hate it."

" But the people here are good people."

" I hate them."

" You ought to go abroad where the people might be more to your liking," suggested Mr. Beck. " You'd like America."

" I hate Americans."

" Why ? "

She thought hard. " Because they wear such ugly knickerbockers—the tourists here."

" The child ! " he thought. " The touching innocence ! "

They were now going by a long country lane that stretched across a lonely field of snow. Far away an engine whistled. The snow hung heavily on the trees. Mr. Beck conceived the plan of approach by way of her father. "I do love the way your father speaks —these little movements of the hands, this fumbling pause, this seeking after the right word. He is by far the most considerable intellectual in the city."

"Yes, Papa is very clever."

They came out into an open space at the mouth of the river which extended wide into the distance, chained in ice. "This is our castle." At the top of a hill surrounded by a fence stood the castle—looking rather less than a mere house. Irmgard quickly vanished up the steps. Mr. Beck stood still a while. The ice-chained river was bathed in moonlight.

There was an added warmth that winter evening about the sky and moon as he walked home to his *pension*.

& III

THE night after he met the Schulzs at the concert in the City Hall. Herr Schulz always sat in the first row and championed foreign artists and blamed his own. That night the Russian Cossacks, visiting the

city for two days, were giving a concert, and he presented them with an autograph copy of his book
The God Triumphant, and made a speech to them,
sprinkling it with words that came most readily and,
as he thought, appropriately to his lips : " Gorki
... Tolstoy ... Dostoëvski ... the great Russian
soul..." During the first interval they all sat down
to refreshments. Herr Schulz held out his glass without
a word. His daughter filled it.

After the concert they walked together down the
slippery street, drifting along with a crowd of Herr
Schulz's admirers, in particular two middle-aged
ladies, to whom Herr Schulz took the opportunity
of presenting the new arrival from America. They
seemed to hang upon every word that issued from
the master—the master expatiating on the concert
with his customary little gestures and taking off his
hat and waving it to right and left, in acknowledgment
of innumerable greetings.

" You have a lot of acquaintances," Mr. Beck
remarked.

" Yes, a lot of acquaintances, but not a single friend !
—I come out with such aphorisms quite spontaneously,
you know. *Ach !* if, like Goethe, I had an Eckermann
to take them down ! As it is, they are not taken down

and are forgotten. Ah, wait a bit : the other day a splendid aphorism occurred to me : ' The only decent people nowadays are to be found among the Jews.' "

" Come, try another ! " the American commented to himself.

" Or this morning—' What we call morality is merely envy.' "

" H'm." There was a pause. " He was a great man—Goethe," uttered Mr. Beck.

" Goethe was—I once put it so well—Goethe was the illegitimate child of the gods."

" And Schiller ? "

" Schiller was a fallen angel who, through a faultless life on earth, has redeemed his fall and secured his amnesty."

" And Shakespeare ? "

" Shakespeare—Shakespeare——" the Director fumbled. " Shakespeare——" It was clear that he was forced this time to make it up on the spot. " Shakespeare is a huge black angel."

" Try another ! " the American reflected.

" Shakespeare——! " Herr Schulz suddenly became excited. " It's incredible." He walked up and down. He waved his hat high in the air as if acknowledging the greetings of acquaintances (who were not there), then stopped dead. " It's—it's—it's beyond words. *King Lear. Antony and Cleopatra. Hamlet.* It's—it's —it's——"

" And Goethe too," the American took up gratefully.

" Yes, Goethe ! What a life the fellow had, long, rich, and complete. And he was understood. Goethe had Schiller. But I am alone : I have nobody."

In bed, Mr. Beck pictured the wedding. Her dad showing off to advantage. What a splendid old fellow ! Then the honeymoon, the bridal night, the return to her parents, the departure for the United States. Their married life when she would get used to him and find in him a vessel for her tenderest outpourings : when she would take him by the hand and, looking frankly in his eyes, would say :

" Mackintosh, I love you."

Through his mind flashed pictures of travel, hotels in the hills, of evenings together, and kisses, caresses and love. And life seemed wonderful and miraculous and full of exquisite anticipations.

& IV

WHEN next day he went to Gmunden, he was stopped in the street by a lady whom he recognised as one of the two middle-aged disciples of Herr Schulz, to whom he had been presented after the concert. " Have you, Herr von Mackintosh, come to see the Herr Direktor Schulz ? " she asked.

Mr. Beck had come to have a quiet view of Gmunden. But he did not deem it polite to say so, and answered, haltingly, " M-yes—I think I have."

" Splendid ! The Herr Direktor is now taking his after-dinner nap, but he will be up for coffee at a quarter past four o'clock and would be delighted to have you take a cup with him."

" Curse him ! " he thought. But at a quarter past four Mr. Beck was at the green, freshly painted gate of a beautiful white villa, trying hard to open the latch from inside, and Herr Schulz, just up from his nap, was coming smilingly down the steps in his pale-yellow boots to Mr. Beck's assistance. He wore a coloured jersey with a plain back to it, and no coat, so that if you looked at him from behind, his shoulders appeared like gigantic epaulets, and there was something which suggested a field-marshal in his colossal bulk. They settled down to coffee in the over-heated glass veranda, the two ladies watching every movement of his brow. " Have you had a good sleep, Herr Direktor ? " they inquired in unison.

" Yes."

There was a pause.

" Yes," he repeated, " I have had a good sleep."

" That's good."

Herr Schulz sighed. " Creative work is very exhausting. It's not the same as giving a lecture. It's work of the spirit and must be spun out of your own soul's substance, so to speak. That's what I keep telling the professors here—he, he ! " he laughed maliciously.

" Entirely so," agreed Mr. Beck. Odd : all the time that the other was talking he could see through his pretence and laugh inwardly ; yet Mr. Beck's replies were sincerely respectful.

" I don't mince words. I tell the professors here straight what I think of them—he, he ! They don't like me."

" No wonder," said the guest, instinctively falling into line with the commanding personality of the other.

" At the heat of creative work I can't write, and so

I dictate my thoughts to this lady here. I wish to goodness, Grete," he turned towards the younger of the ladies, " that you would learn to use a typewriter." He held out his cup : the lady filled it. " To attempt to read your hand is insufferable. How do you, Herr Doktor Mackintosh, do your work—Ethnology is your subject, I think you told me ?—do you use a typewriter ? "

" I've an Underwood Portable—it's quite small."

" H'm. I don't think I could ever use a small typewriter. I should want something big and solid by way of a typewriter."

" Yes ! Yes ! " the two sisters exclaimed ecstatically. " You must have everything big and solid, Herr Direktor, to express your personality."

" He, he ! " he laughed, and turning to the guest —" These ladies are hero-worshippers," he explained.

" The Herr Direktor is always making fun of us," they said, and looked at him adoringly.

" Perhaps if you will kindly follow me upstairs it might be of interest to you to see the room where some of the more significant strands of thought have occurred to me of a morning. Sophie and Grete come in and draw the blinds open for me when I ring. I let the sun shine in my eyes, and as I lie in bed all the morning, I think—God! the wonderful things that come into one's head at these times. *Ach !*...My family are jealous of these ladies because I spend so much time here. But I can't work at home, with my wife and fourteen children in the house and the telephone going, doors banging. As I said to my wife when I left the house the other day, in protest: 'It's not the *fact* of the door banging which upsets me. No: it's the brazen thoughtlessness *behind* the act, the invidious ignorance of the effect of such a bang upon an intellectual worker.' That's what drives me away from home to seek my real ' I ' in solitude amid nature. Here I have peace. The ladies are so kind and thoughtful. It costs me nothing. They are only too glad to have me, and my company, they say, amply compensates them for whatever food I may consume here. Here I feel I can work. The sun shines in my window till I get up for dinner at two o'clock. After dinner I take a little nap on this tiny balcony till about a quarter past four, when I go down to coffee. After coffee— this reminds me—I take a little walk—you must come with me—till supper-time. H'm. We might as well go now."

They went down the steps, Herr Schulz breathing heavily upon the nape of the visitor's neck, who, turning round, asked, " Do you do most of your work after supper then ? "

" No. I turn in early. Creative work is very exhausting. After supper we have a little game of chess —and then we all turn in."

" I see you do your writing in the morning, in bed ? "

There was a pause. " I have ideas buzzing in my head for a novel, a play—a philosophical work. But what I lack is the *inner* freedom. I am upset by the invidious perversity of the people around me, by the perfidious, shameless, iniquitous meanness of mankind ! "

Grete met them at the foot of the stairs. " I suppose, Herr von Mackintosh, that you're an American journalist who has come over to Europe to acquaint himself with the life and works of Herr Direktor Schulz ? "

" Well—perhaps—yes—though of course——" mumbled the visitor.

Herr Schulz now stood half turned away from them with his hands behind his back, brooding.

" I should be glad," said he, turning back to them suddenly, " if you, Herr Doktor Mackintosh, would acquaint the people of America—for whom, I assure you, I cherish the warmest regard (their achievements in technical knowledge are most valuable, I am sure, and are a significant contribution to mechanical progress)—if you would acquaint them with my writings and works and...if you would be so kind," he concluded.

" Gladly."

" For I must confess that I do not expect much recognition at the hands of my own people—the professors especially. I have even coined a good aphorism about these gentlemen—' officials of science,' I call them—he, he ! They don't like me. It's nothing new, of course. There is even the proverb : ' No man is a hero to his own valet '—I rather meant another proverb : ' No man is a prophet in his own country.' "

" Pardon me, Herr Direktor, but will you be good enough to acquaint me with the titles of your works."

Herr Schulz suddenly grew earnest. " There is that—*God Triumphant*—you know that. Or—I beg your pardon—I will send you a copy of it when I get home. Then—there are one or two little—well, youthful attempts—school essays. Since I left the bank two years ago I have not been able to do anything at all. I lack the inner freedom."

" No matter. With us it's not so much the work as the personality that counts. And that, I can assure you,

you have in ample measure. You even, if you will pardon me for saying so, remind me of Henrik Ibsen."

" Of Björnson," corrected Herr Schulz. " Ibsen was small—insignificant-looking. But Björnson was a man after my own face and stature—he, he ! "

" Yes ! Yes ! " chimed in the ladies. " The image of Björnson ! "

" Though some people say I look rather like an English lord—he, he ! "

Mr. Beck had never seen an English lord and did not know what a lord exactly looked like : but he knew he did not look like Herr Direktor Schulz. He gazed at the Director as he stood there with the " epaulets." He *was* a great man ; there was no doubt about it when you looked at him—six foot six and two full spans between the shoulders !

" I shall now leave the two gentlemen to themselves," said Grete. " They have doubtless important matters to discuss which are not for a woman's poor mind."

" We shall be back for supper, Grete," rejoined Herr Schulz, " which I trust we shall enjoy the better after our walk."

" I will do my best that it may come up to your expectation, Herr Direktor." And the two men went through the garden into the adjacent wood,

Herr Schulz breaking off dead branches (an easy enough job, the visitor reflected) as if to bear out the impression that he was, in every respect, a colossus. " You are lucky," he said. " You're still young, independent, can do your work without interruption. But I—I try to keep it down, but bitterness—bitterness rises here in my breast against—against people—debts, petty tyrannies—the invidious meanness, the iniquitous perfidy of mankind ! " Herr Schulz broke off a dead branch. " If I had some great sorrow, I would rise to the occasion, like a tragic hero—a King Lear, let us say—with credit and glory. But no ! These petty, senseless little pinpricks—the telephone ringing while I am composing a lyric, the door slamming away— these pinpricks...these— these dirty little setbacks..."

Mr. Beck looked sympathetic. " I understand. Even Tartarin de Tarascon used to say : *Des coups d'épée! des coups d'épée, messieurs! mais pas des coups d'épingle ! "*

" Don't know. Haven't read him." He stopped, and suddenly, from habit, though no one was about, took off and waved his hat high in the air, as if acknowledging the greeting of somebody behind the trunk of the tree, then put it back on his head. " While I am trying hard to mount Pegasus I am pulled down

129

ignominiously by the breeches, so to speak, because they come to tell me that baby has choked himself with orange pips. My wife has given birth to fourteen children. I ask : What can a poet do ? "

" Exactly. On that ground I am in favour of Eugenics."

" What ! " Herr Schulz broke off a dead branch. " You are in favour of that—that invidious—that— that infamous practice. You——"

" I am. I have a nightmare : over-population."

Herr Schulz pooh-poohed this statement. " Non- sense ! Look,"—his eye was searching forward past the densely growing trees ; he pointed to an empty meadow,—" Look : plenty of standing room."

" I am thinking," the American pursued, " of the poor women who bear child after child without respite."

" It's their business."

" But surely, Herr Direktor, there is many a wife who does not want any children. What are you to do with such a woman ? "

" Fling her out of the window," was the advice. " No, no, Herr Doktor Mackintosh, it's no good arguing. My wife has had eleven children by me and three by my predecessor. I have no money.

Being honest, I retired, a poor man. I am creaking under a burden of debt. But I won't stop. I will not contradict the will of God. And my old woman knows better than to show signs of unnatural reluctance. She knows her man—he, he!"

"But don't the children get to be weaklings?"

"Not a bit of it. My youngest boy, who is only two, is the cleverest of the lot. I can talk to him as I do to you. Though naturally," the Director hastened, "he hasn't got your knowledge. Ethnology is your subject, is it not?"

"Quite so."

"Of course."

"And your daughters, Herr Direktor?" Mr. Beck thought this might be the chance to ask Herr Schulz for the hand of Irmgard, though, on second thoughts, he resolved that it would be wiser to approach the daughter first.

"My daughters are not quite so clever. But then what can you expect of mere women? Though, Irmgard is awakening. She has vague unfocussed longings...."

"That reminds me," chimed in the guest. "I have been reading recently the correspondence between Goethe and Schiller. There is a passage where Goethe speaks of Spring: 'I have an objectless sorrow in Spring....'"

"I too," said Herr Schulz. "*Ach!* when I look at the hills and the lakes and the breaking rigour of the sky, I want—I want to go *praying* through the world!"

"Entirely so," said the other.

They were returning to the villa, and Grete was waiting for them on the steps. "All's ready," she smiled dotingly.

&V

AND now Frau von Kranich began inviting him: "*Please komme on Fryday next at 4 o'klock P.M. We will go together to Wolfs.*" Or, "*Please komme on Thursday at 3 o'klock P.M. We will go to Schmidts.*" Presently he had another letter:

"*Miss Schulz is just staying with me und whishes me to invite you for next Thursday to komme to the castle at 4 o'klock P.M. Then she advises you further to take dansing lessons by Herr Loewe to learn Wienerwalzer. I hope you don't think me forward. If so, I beg your pardon. With her und my best compliments, Yours truly, Emmy von Kranich.*"

Next morning there was another missive. Across

132

a visiting card on which stood " Emmy von Kranich, née von Kolbe," she wrote : " *You are geting with this an invitation for a closed society fancy dress to which Miss Schulz will also komme. She is kounting on you beeing there because you are to acompany her home. Yours truly.*"

When on Thursday he set out for the Schulzs', he walked as it seemed to him a deuced long way, until at last the river spread wide before him and he perceived the castle on the hill, looking rather less than a mere house. He went up the winding path, till in the annexe on the second floor (the castle had been commandeered during the war and ever since the Schulzs could not get the lodgers out) he rang the bell and waited, while his heart thumped loud within him. It was Irmgard herself who opened the door for him—Irmgard in a dark-blue velvet dress which she might have worn when she was still fifteen, and her hair he noticed, was put up for the first time. As he entered the drawing-room (which, for lack of space, served also as a dining-room, and, in fact, as a study for the Herr Direktor at such rare times as he was at home : to-day he wasn't) the mother of the fourteen children rose to greet him—a woman remarkably fresh for her achievement. On a pedestal stood a huge bronze bust of Herr Schulz, and on the shelf behind, two small busts—

of Goethe and Schiller. There was a moment of confused silence. Mr. Beck surveyed the view through the window and expressed ravishment in no measured terms. A tiny little boy of two came in. " This is Karl, our youngest," said Frau Schulz. And Irmgard, to give herself something to do—for she seemed very shy, Mr. Beck felt, at this overt arrival of the first grown man who had come expressly for her sake— took her little brother on her lap and screened her face with him from the visitor. But tight as she held him, he managed to crawl off and whispered something into his mother's ear.

" No, the Herr Doktor is not interested to see your horse," she rejoined aloud.

" Oh, but I am ! " And by the mother's pleasant smile he felt that he had thus commended himself to her heart.

" Well, fetch it then," she said to Karl, who vanished; and presently there came a scratching, squealing noise from the adjoining room, and Karl dragged in on a long string a cadaverous moth-eaten rocking horse and began taking off the saddle in front of the visitor, who patted it to gain time, while thinking hard of what he might say next. He had an agreeable feeling of being taken straight into the heart of the family.

Mother and daughter had fixed their eyes on Karl
and Mr. Beck, who as it were made a tableau together,
and the guest ransacked his mind for something at
once appropriate and amusing to say to Karl. But—
" Can you strap the saddle to the head ? " was all he
could produce. The little boy, evidently not amused,
gravely repudiated the suggestion. Irmgard got up
and busied herself with the tea-things. Her mother's
glance followed her fondly. " You can't guess, Herr
Doktor, what Irmgard will be wearing at the fancy-
dress ball ! "

" No, no ! " cried the girl. " You mustn't tell or
he'll recognise me ! "

On the piano lid stood a family group which attracted Mr. Beck's attention—*padre, madre,* and fourteen
bambini : twelve girls, two boys. " This is Hellmut,
our grown-up brother. He is twenty-nine."

" H'm. A good-looking youth," commented the
visitor.

" He used to be good-looking. But a year ago
in tobogganing down the hill he banged with his nose
into a tree and ever since his nose is twice its former
size. I always tease him about his double nose."

" How very funny ! "

The hours flashed by like lightning. The window

135

grew dim. The maid came in, lit the lamp and drew the curtains. The hostess looked as though she thought that Mr. Beck ought to go now. But Mr. Beck sat still, and did not move.

"Irmgard is going to town now to a dancing lesson at Herr Loewe's. She feels a little out-of-date and wants to regain confidence before the dance to-morrow," Frau Schulz imparted to the lingering guest.

"You can come with me," said Irmgard, "and arrange with Loewe about your *Wienerwalzer* lessons."

They went down the endless road, Irmgard smiling to herself. She called in at several shops—" Just wait outside, will you ? " He noticed through the glass door how the men behind the counter stared at her with rapture, and he felt proud of being—even if compelled to wait outside—her immediate companion. "Now we can go to Loewe's," she said—and sighed. And at that sigh, consummative of their arduous day's work, he felt a thrill—and also sighed. "Now I should ask her," he told himself, but they were crossing the main street and dodging vehicles, and now already they were at Herr Loewe's door. He watched her take her lesson, Herr Loewe, as he held her in his practised arms, smiling all the while into her eyes. And when she left, Herr Loewe exercised him for an hour and a half in the whirling motions of the *Wiener-walzer*, charged him a hundred thousand crowns and instructed him to come again to-morrow.

On the way to Herr Loewe's next day, he called on Frau von Kranich. " Mind the lamp," she drawled. But Mr. Beck had already knocked his scalp against the pike of the brass fitting, and so sat down, feeling a little stunned, facing the old dame. " He, he, he— you are so tall," she laughed, and looked at him in a strange way, as if to ask : " Is it coming off all right ? " Mr. Beck responded with a look of joyous confidence. And she said, " We may soon be able to congratulate you ?—he, he, he ! "

" I hope so," he responded, rising and once more knocking his head against the lamp.

" Mind ! " said Frau von Kranich. She sat there in a soft armchair, with feet resting on a cushion, and smiled before her faintly—an old, old, white-haired woman with one foot already in the grave.

" What's this ? " he asked striding over to the wall.

" A miniature of my mother as a young woman at the time my father was Bavarian Minister at Rome."

Herr Loewe that day had hired two girls to spin Mr. Beck round, and, clad in his new cut-away, with his tails in the air, he went round and round, till one girl was fagged out and the other took him on and whirled on with him till he felt faint and the blood rushed to his eyes.

"Come now, beat the time with the right heel," Herr Loewe admonished relentlessly. Mr. Beck spun round in a pink faint and reflected that his suffering must be endured for love's sake.

"Now you're all right," Herr Loewe absolved him, more kindly, pocketing another hundred-thousand-crown note. "The secret, remember, lies in beating the time with the right heel."

On his way home, his heart thumping irregularly after the lesson, he thought: "Am I too old for her? Can girls like Irmgard really begin to love middle-aged men like myself?" The tailor had brought the new dinner-jacket and retired: "Have the honour—kiss the hand—greet God—commend myself—my compliment," and as he was putting on his new clothes he whistled: "I, Mackintosh J. Beck, am taking out the prettiest girl in Europe!" He shaved with especial care, and beheld his face and his entire figure in the looking-glass with genuine satisfaction. Walking through the sloppy streets—it seemed that spring was already beginning—he remembered a bet with a college chum at home. The first of them to be engaged was to send the other a cheque for fifty dollars. He imagined his chum opening the envelope. He pictured how he would arrive in America with his young wife, how he would spite the dark-eyed Susy who had broken with him just because he happened to prefer the company of her intellectual brother to her own.

Schindler at last. All shake hands and introduce themselves, the Secretary in addition presenting Mr. Beck right and left as "Mister Captain Mackintosh." He waits at the door. She comes in at last, dressed as a butterfly and wearing a black mask with a tilted nose. It was cold in the room and she twitched her nude girlish shoulders.

" I recognised you straight away."

She looked a little sulky. Or was it the black mask that made her look so? The mother smiled sorrowfully. " I said he'd recognise you straight away if we went in together."

" I'm afraid this is not a very good table," said the cavalier, escorting them.

" It will do," said the girl.

" Why so sulky ? "

" I was so before we left."

" Why ? "

" Oh, never mind."

The waiter came up. " What will you have ? "

" Nothing yet."

Remembering what Frau von Kranich said,—" You ought to have come not as a butterfly, but as Cinderella," he ventured.

Her mouth smiled behind the mask, but the eyes still looked defiant. " Oh, yes, while I remember——" The mother was fumbling in her bag, and presently produced from there a copy of *The God Triumphant* with a huge brown man with a broken nose upon the cover, and duly autographed inside. " My husband sends you this, with his respectful compliments."

" Oh, thanks—" Mr. Beck was peeping furtively into the pages, and—" It's a great book," he gave his grateful verdict.

" Yes, not everyone can understand it," agreed the author's wife.

Through her black mask with the unbecoming tilted nose Irmgard's eyes glared angrily, defiantly, and he wondered what precisely was the matter. When the waiter came again, she would have nothing. When he came a third time, she would have nothing. When he came a fourth time, Irmgard said, abruptly, that she would have lemonade. Mr. Beck suggested wine, and she said she would have none, and Mr. Beck, thinking she was sorry for his pocket, hastened to suggest light-heartedly that Tokai wine was very nice and sweet. " I know Tokai wine," she said, in a tone implying that it was certainly as familiar to her as to himself. " But I don't want it."

After that Mr. Beck sat silent for a while. And the waiter brought the lemonade. She sipped at it once, and then did not touch it again. The waitress came along with the cakes. " Will you have some ? " he ventured.

But she shook her head and sighed. He looked at the mother, and the mother cast a sympathetic look at her. " Cheer up. He may come yet."

The girl did not answer. Mr. Beck thought that he must on no account whatever miss the moment of proposing to her. " Shall I now ? " But at the sight of her defiant eyes he let his head drop on his chest : and, behold ! he noticed, with dismay, that he had dropped pieces of the sticky chocolate-cream cake upon his trousers, and thinking this was possibly the reason why she was angry, he began to scratch it off, tentatively, with his finger-nail. She averted her glance, still looking angry ; and thinking that *this* was then why she was angry, he stopped scratching. Mother and daughter exchanged vague glances. " But to-morrow he is sure to come."

" Yes, I think he'll come to-morrow," said the girl —and looked more friendly.

Mr. Beck rose. " May I have this dance ? " She got up, without answering him, and adjusting her butterfly wings which hung down from her wrists, came into his arms, and they glided away cautiously and not too confidently. " Shall I now ? " But he had to concentrate his attention on manœuvring her past other couples, while she seemed very frightened of making a mistake, and it was a relief to them both when the music stopped and they returned to the mother. " A bad floor," said Mr. Beck.

" Yes, the floor is not good."

" Do take off your mask."

She shook her head.

Mr. Beck did not dance the next dance, nor the one after. Nor did a single cavalier come up to her.

" Oh, come, take off that mask ! " her mother urged at last.

Irmgard shook her head. A minute elapsed ; and she took off the mask.

No sooner had she done so than a cavalier was at her side, then a second, a third, a fourth, a tenth.

Introductions—Herr Baron——, Herr Graf——. All
the impecunious aristocracy of Austria was wooing
her virginal charms. Irmgard brightened up. She
danced. "What a beautiful girl!" "What an exquisite face!" said the old fogies surveying her. They
wished they could dance too, but their dancing was
of the old school : alas ! they were ignorant of the jazz.

But at last the conductor held up his *bâton* more
defiantly—and it went off, the old ever-popular waltz
On the Beautiful Blue Danube. All the old fogies, who
had so far languished in obscure corners, crawled out,
like beetles, at the sound of the first bars, and went
spinning round on their axes, to the large, deliberate
rhythm. Mr. Beck wanted to try his luck, but before
he could open his mouth Irmgard was off, whirling
round with Baron Karl Franz Egon Gaestner zu
Hauch Wolf-Kadelburg von Hofmannsthal. Mr. Beck
looked at her complexion. It was perfect as in a child,
and the nose shone slightly. Clearly she hadn't even
begun to use powder.

Elated by her sudden success, Irmgard wanted to go
to Herr Loewe's dance next door. She was impatient
—could not wait for the cloak-room ticket—could not
wait till Mr. Beck had got back his change. She danced
with him, excited by the stares which she received from

every side, drunk with success. " Now let's walk," she said, taking his arm.

" This is the time," he thought. " Still one can't very well barge into it like that. One ought to tell her something about oneself," he argued with himself ; and opportunely said : " You hardly know anything about my life and work. I must seem a stranger to you —a blank signifying nothing. And yet I've written some standard works in Ethnology and am of some account in that branch of science."

" You must write in German if I am to read them," she replied. " Now we must rush back."

At that " we " he felt unusually intimate, and he said as he helped her on with her coat, " Turn up your collar," and even turned it up for her, at which she frowned. " Now for it ! " he thought.

" I want to tell you something."

" Afterwards," she said, and rushed away from him back to her mother.

He walked with them to the castle. At the injunction of the mother Irmgard did not speak and held her shawl close to the chin. When he went to bed it was past five o'clock.

& VI

THE night after he joined them at the dance in the
City Hall. It seemed that the entrance ticket had
already been provided for him by the girl. But when,
pocket-book in hand, he was about to give her the
money, she flared up—" Don't give it me here ! "

And he smarted. When he came up to her in the
ball-room he saw that she was red and angry, standing
with her brother Hellmut with the double nose,
who was also red and angry. They could not secure
an empty table and stood in the draughty doorway,
jammed by the crowd. " Will you put this into your
pocket ? " She handed him her little vanity bag. The
band struck up a *Wienerwalzer*, and he asked her.
It didn't go as well as it should have done, after two
lessons. " Beat the time with the right heel," he
remembered Herr Loewe's injunction. And he *did* beat
it, and with the right heel. Only he could not get it
exactly in time, and the left heel came down of itself
just as the right one was due, every time. They had only
done a few paces. " No, that won't do," she said,
releasing him.

Two lessons gone for naught ! However that may be,

he must not miss the chance—perhaps the last—of proposing to her : " Shall I now ? "

But she looked angry. Her (father's) small eyes looked angry, as if at the perfidious meanness, the invidious perversity of mankind. Her sister Elsa's fiancé, a young man employed at the local circus, was making funny little signs to Irmgard, to amuse her. But she never looked. Mr. Beck gave up talking to her.

" Ah ! Mister Captain Mackintosh ! " A man whom he had met the night before came up to him and, taking him by the arm, imparted to him that he was looking for a certain Dr. Schmidt. And for an hour Mr. Beck was dragged about all round the rooms and through the vestibule and down the restaurant and up the stairs all round the gallery, in search of the elusive Dr. Schmidt whom he had never seen nor even wished to see. They did not find Dr. Schmidt ; and it is to be presumed that Mr. Beck died without seeing him ; but he killed, however disagreeably and unprofitably, one hour of his mental agony.

Exhausted, he sat down in the gallery and watched the crowded ball-room heave in whirling couples to the mighty rhythms of the *Danube Waltz*. The big orchestra put a dashing emphasis into the lusty, regularly whirling strains. " For you the hesitant irregu-

larities of jazz : for us the regular abandon of the
Wienerwalzer," these whirling sounds and faces seemed
to sing aloft. And behold, a military figure holding
in his martial arms a slim fair lady, went round and round,
tapping the time with his right heel. And there
again—an elderly couple : they had placed their hands
on each other's shoulders at arms' length and went
round, the man tapping his heel. A post-office official
whirled round with his girl, his face all of a smile.
These multitudinous couples did not bang into one
another as often as one might expect. Like so many
spinning tops, they each turned on their particular
axis, just clearing each other, while the music lashed
them on into a frenzied passion of regular rhythm. Mr.
Beck leaned forward, watching down into the vulgar
opulence of the gilded ball-room stunned, fallen into
a trance or reverie. And the conglomeration for some
reason recalled to him those crowded frescoes packed
with human figures that one sees in Botticelli. Away,
away was the post-office official. And there, nearing his
end of the room, was Irmgard, the peri, the nymph !

When at length he returned to the joint table,
Irmgard was not there ; it seemed as if she avoided
him. Mr. Beck caught a sentence which had passed
between Elsa and her fiancé : " It's too late—he won't

come now. Poor Irmgard!" The betrothed young couple took pity on the lonely Mr. Beck and, with the aid of another young couple, got him to join in a complicated dance in which Mr. Beck had to describe elaborate, intricate figures with his tired legs—and felt like a fool. Irmgard, with an angry frown, danced with a pale young man with a pinched look. Mr. Beck paced round alone, pulling out his watch and rehearsing mentally how, in parting, he would thank the betrothed young couple for their kindness to him and hand Irmgard back her vanity bag without a word—and go. They talked of wanting to go on to a coffee-house to drink coffee in the morning, by way of doing justice to the *Fasching*, but Mr. Beck only wanted to get into bed and to calm his poor nerves. The hours dragged. It was four; then it was five—but still the dancing went on. At last he buttonholed the circus man. " I want to go home," he pleaded wearily.

"No, no! We're staying on till six. Surely, Herr von Mackintosh, you don't want to be guilty of ruining our little Carnival party?"

Mr. Beck did not want to ruin anything and, as a cultivated man in foreign parts, deemed it only right not to do anything which might cause them in their own poor light, to think him ill-mannered. So he paced on by himself round and round (he was afraid that if he sat down he might fall asleep), now and then pulling out his watch and yawning into his white-cuffed hand. The clock struck half-past seven. It struck eight o'clock. Somebody was making a collection for the band, and spoke : " If we pay them they'll play on till nine." A sleepy waiter looked angrily at Mr. Beck. " All d-ham foolishness ! " said he, evidently recognising an American in him. " All d-ham foolishness ! The lights are only paid for till half-past eight." He was falling over from fatigue ; his eyes were closing of themselves. He was a tottering figure in the corner. Mr. Beck was still pacing about waiting eagerly for the Schulzs to make a start— when suddenly he ran into the circus man. " The ladies have just gone home with their brother Hellmut and asked me to say good-bye for them."

" What ! They've gone ? "

He was staggered by the news—his heart all weeping tears. In the large vestibule there was a draught, and as he pressed his way through the crowd, Mr. Mackintosh Beck felt all nasty inside—as if he had just arrived at the Hook of Holland after a particularly vile crossing from Harwich. While waiting for his coat and hat in the icy cloak-room with the doors swinging to and fro, he had a chilly feeling in his bosom, as though some improvident maid had left open all windows and doors ; and a tremendous draught swept the length and breadth of his inner rooms. When he came out of the City Hall it was morning, and a round white mist stood on the sharp mountain edge, like an enormous balloon. The snow fell in heaps; it seemed as though a new winter spell were beginning. He shivered in his coat and felt a dull ache in the pit of his stomach. As he walked home it was bitterly cold, and a sharp wind blew from across the river. And suddenly it seemed as if the mountains pressed their awful weight upon his chest, stifling his breath, so that he could have screamed in anguish—rapped his heart....

He could feel the vanity bag in his side-pocket and thought: " That girl ought to be whipped!" And to be treated like that by a mere *Backfisch* ! It came over him—the urgent wish to press all his latent claims to renown upon her. Impudent nincompoop! The tears in his throat rolled back at this rebellious thought. He shaped in his mind the letter he would write to Frau von Kranich : " I return the vanity bag which—— I am sorry that your good intentions have involved me——" No, that would never do. " Of all the rude

girls that I have ever met——" No, no, that might
lead to unpleasantness, who knows ? Suddenly her
brother Hellmut with the swollen double nose rose
before him, threatening. Mr. Beck did not know for a
fact whether Hellmut had been a student and so
was a ready hand at sword-duelling. He assumed,
nevertheless, that Herr Direktor Schulz, despite
his record, had not begrudged his son a university
education, seeing how extraordinarily cheap it was
on the continent of Europe. He could not remember
having seen any sword cuts on Hellmut's face. But
he recalled the swollen double nose, which, though
no direct indication of unusual ferocity, yet did argue
a certain dare-devilry, a love of courting danger—
which well might mean danger for Mr. Mackintosh
Beck. " Damn ! " he thought, " blast the whole
bally crew of them ! "

He pictured the duel, the rising in the cold early
morning—a sword in his vitals—his death. " No,"
he thought, " the girl isn't worth it ! "

Suddenly he felt old, too old to take on such risks.
He understood that young girls like Irmgard could
not love men like himself. He crossed the bridge,
and slowly began the ascent to his *pension*. It was
still snowing, and the sky looked bleak, solitary,

senseless. And he thought : " I am glad ; I am glad."

Going back to his room—all upside down from the erewhile ardour of dressing—he remembered how he had looked forward to both nights and had dressed with particular care. It had seemed to him then that he looked very smart. Now the new dinner-jacket looked loose, the shirt crumpled, the new patent leather shoes cracked. He sat down at the table and saw his face in the glass : it was sallow, haggard as though he had been travelling for three nights on end without a sleeper. What mental suffering could do ! And the powder on the upper lip had melted away and revealed the red patches from the scraping blade. He noticed that whenever he shaved with particular care it always came out worse. His hair was turning very grey—there was a bald patch on the crown. He remembered how ugly he had looked in the glass at the tailor's—and understood.

And now, with fluttering heart, he opened the vanity bag—a plain little wallet of pink chiffon—and beheld its contents : a pinch of greased powder, sweet-smelling, in a scrap of crumpled paper. And he thought she never powdered ! Two white spotless handkerchiefs with the initial " I " and three little flowers around embroidered in blue silk. In another pocket, a crumpled bit of white paper containing rouge. How touching! And behold! a long hair—Irmgard's. He took it between his fingers and pressed it tight, and it seemed to coil, like a snake, as if alive. And in that cruel, treacherous movement also was Irmgard.

But what was this? A photo of a young good-looking student. Another photo—Irmgard and the student. A third photo—Irmgard, Elsa, Hellmut, and the student. It dawned upon him suddenly how during both nights she had been strangely distracted; he recalled the words and looks that passed between her and her family. He understood: he perfectly understood....

And the whole vanity bag smelt sweetly—like her sweet seventeen. By a simple flash of intuition into her being, he understood how she had moods and a life independent of his, and that it was right that it was so. In this her first Carnival dance, long since prepared for, she had been disappointed, and not the least disappointed in him, and perhaps also was crying now. And suddenly his sight was blurred. He took off his horn-rimmed spectacles and wiped the glass with his big handkerchief....

& VII

NEXT morning he despatched the vanity bag, with a note, to Frau von Kranich, requesting her to hand it to the proper owner, and having done that he felt relieved, and even whistled. When he came back to lunch, he was informed that in his absence Herr Direktor Schulz had telephoned no less than half-a-dozen times, and that Frau von Kranich had also telephoned. " Aha ! " he thought. " They've smelt a rat ! They've got the wind up ! " He remembered the attitude of Frau von Kranich right from the beginning. He recalled the glib, glossy manner of Herr Schulz. A bag of vanity ! What was he after ? What was this indeed ? An attempt at the eleventh hour to enmesh him, an American, into matrimonial entanglements. He pictured how they had prevailed on her, the dollars looming largely in their mind, to give up the student and to accept him before too late. Like a good American, he was afraid of being drawn into the dark jungles and tangles of European affairs —family affairs most of all—and, for the first time in his life, he perceived the deep significance, the traditional sacrosanctity of the Monroe Doctrine of uncompromising isolation and entrenchment. As he finished his soup, the maid came in to say that Herr Direktor Schulz was at the telephone and had also sent up his son with a message of an urgent kind. The blood rushed to his temples. "A plot!" he thought. "A finely laid snare!" Mr. Mackintosh Beck became that most scared of all things—a middle-aged gentleman afraid of being seduced. But he conquered these insidious thoughts. He held fast to his chair and spoke :

"My head is bloody, but unbowed."

He packed in a frenzy, strapping up his bags before he was quite ready, and at the last shoving things into his pockets, and set off to the station, and as he crossed the bridge chucked *The God Triumphant*, unread, into the river. He was pacing the platform, muttering through his teeth—

"It matters not how strait the gate,
　How charged with punishment the scroll ;
　I am the master of my fate,
　I am the captain of my soul,"

when he heard a heavy puffing at his back, and turning, he perceived Herr Schulz in the trilby hat and astrakhan coat (looking like an English lord), striding up to him in his pale-yellow boots. "Herr Doktor Mackintosh!" The man was holding out his arms. "*Ach!* how incredibly glad I am to have caught you!"

"Now he'll begin throwing the girl at me when I don't want her," the American reflected, and steeled his heart, and bowed his head as if to meet the attack. Herr Schulz breathed heavily and wiped his brow. "It's...awful! On the one hand, this lovely weather —these mountains—lakes—the breaking rigour in the sky—when I look at nature I feel—I feel I want to go *praying* through the world! On the other hand, this other life, immediate, extravagant calls on my nervous force." He spoke on, with little wavy movements of the hand. "If I had some great sorrow, by God I would bear it—like a Lucifer, I would bear it! But these petty, senseless, dirty little pinpricks ...setbacks, bills, petty tyrannies, telephone calls, interruptions. At last, I could stand it no longer, I opened the door. When I'm angry I'm like a raging elephant. I'm a big man, and my family know that at such moments I am capable of anything; they are then like frightened mice—he, he! 'I want Herr Doktor Mackintosh!' I shouted. I felt that I must have a kindred soul to talk to—immediately, that very moment—if I was not to suffocate of rage and bitterness which rises—rises and boils here in my breast!

My wife began undoing trunks and boxes, looking, if you please, for my old waterproof! I lost my temper. It's not the act, the absurdity of looking for a raincoat when you crave the presence of a human soul : it's the thought *behind* the act—or rather this sheer thoughtlessness and inattentiveness, this—this invidious meanness and perversity latent in mankind that stabs me. I said : *Herr Doktor* Mackintosh. There was no possible chance of misapprehension. Well, I had them telephone to you all the morning—to Frau von Kranich. They couldn't get you. They can never get anything. I slammed the door and went. Hellmut ran up against me and said they'd told him you had gone straight to the station. And now I'm here. Well, how are you ? Where are you going ? "

" At first to Vienna. Then to Venice, Florence, Rome, Paris, London, and so home *viâ* New York."

Herr Schulz looked at him, and down at his own pale yellow boots, but with a vacant stare, obviously not perceiving either. " We poets need friends. Goethe had Schiller. I have nobody. I am alone, and the divine gift in me is dribbling to no purpose. There are no real people here. The professors—I tell them straight what I think of them—he, he ! They don't

like me. Yes, we need friends. Even little poets,"
Herr Schulz added, unexpectedly.

He listened to Herr Schulz. And he experienced
an agreeable feeling of elation at his self-control. That
he was able, for the first time, to shelve his love and
give attention to those other matters proved to him
that he was stronger than his love, not then suspecting
that, perhaps, his love itself had temporarily abated.
" Been doing any work ? " he asked.

" I have ideas," said Herr Schulz, " for a novel, a
satirical epic, a play—a series of short stories. But——"
He looked accusingly at Mr. Beck.

" I know."

Mr. Beck stood speechless, thinking hard what he
could say. " Your book was wonderful," he said at
length.

" It was very well received."

The guards were already slamming the doors,
and Mr. Beck stepped inside, and let down the window
and shook hands with Herr Schulz. The whistle went.
The train moved. And Herr Schulz, waving his hat
high in the air, his long silver locks flying grotesquely
in the wind, receded and glided away.

" *She* had not stirred at all then...." He felt a mild
pang for his pride. He had adjusted his things on the

rack. It was hot in the compartment, but he had not yet taken off his coat because the old lady next him was sitting on his coat buttons. Past glided the long yellow building, the barracks, the hills, the Café Schindler, the City Hall, the river—towers and pinnacles. " All the same," he reflected, " I think I like the old duffer best."